Lovers

Hiatus

"Vacation Love Series"

Taylor Love

Taylor Made Day Dreams
Bringing an "imaginative break" to your day!

Lovers Hiatus

Copyright © 2019 by Taylor Love

This is a work of fiction. Names, characters, places and incidents are either the product of the author's imagination or are used fictitiously, and any resemblance to actual persons, living or dead, business establishments, events or locales is entirely coincidental.

To the extent that the image or images on the cover of this book depict a person or persons, such person or persons are merely models. This book is for adult readership and may contain adult situations, language and sexual content.

Dedication

My fifth novel might come off as a personal fantasy, so I guess this is dedicated to me! Two writers trapped together and passion overtakes them, it could happen! Makes me want to book some writing retreats. Also, a look into the minds of writers as a whole. Many people think this is an "easy, quick" process. For most writers, it's far from it. Some are wracked with self-doubt daily, while other's creative process stalls out due to the many stressors of life. Not to mention for some it's a labor of love that can take mere months to several years before a book is finished. It like any other job—takes hard work, dedication, a thick skin *and* is often underappreciated.

About the Author

Taylor Love is a Michigan Author who writes Sexy-Modern-Romance books that focus primarily on Black on Black Love stories, that are sweet, romantic, steamy and positive. I prefer my books overall to have low "drama" and stick to the "journey" of two people meeting and over time falling in love. Of course, with the pitfalls and ups and downs that entails. My goal is to tell interesting contemporary, realistic (to a certain degree—as who doesn't love a little "make-believe") romance stories for African American's around the world. My books should pair well with the mature-minded reader who wants to see relationships done in a non-dysfunctional way and a glass of your favorite wine! Black romantic love is real!

Instant Chemistry Series
Running Into You
Not My Type
One Click For Love

A Instant Chemistry Novella
In Between Chemistry

Vacation Love Series
Crashing In On Love
Lovers Hiatus

Instant Chemistry Shorts
Cam & Andrea-New Years Eve
Cam & Andrea-Don't Forget What you Have At Home
Robert & Mika-Weekend With The Lordes

Stay In Touch!
Facebook- https://www.facebook.com/TaylorMadeDayDreams/
Newsletter- (No Spam) http://eepurl.com/duB-Fn
Twitter- https://twitter.com/TaylorLoveWrite
Instagram- https://www.instagram.com/taylorlovewriter/
Bookbub- https://www.bookbub.com/profile/taylor-love

Prologue

Janae had been driving through no man's land for over four hours, but in the last thirty minutes snow had started falling from the sky. Guess it could have been worse, and she had almost reached Michigan's first city.

Sault Ste. Marie here I come!

She wanted to be excited but honestly on this first day of January she felt just as she had yesterday—uninspired. But that was okay, the entire reason for this trip was to rectify that. When the phone rang she started not to take it, until she saw it was her cousin. Clicking her hands-free earpiece on she figured why not, it wasn't like there was much to look at beside the trees anyway.

"Hey Shella, what's up? I can't talk long I'm driving, and it just started to snow."

"Hey cus! I won't keep you. I'm in line waiting to get on my cruise ship...in Spain!"

"Wait, what?" Janae laughed, thinking Shella was playing. Besides herself, Shella was the *least* spontaneous person she knew.

"You heard me. That's why I'm calling so someone will know where I'm at. I emailed you the details. I'll be gone for six weeks."

"Are you crazy?"

"No more crazier than you, going up into "no black-people land" by *yourself*. For two months. In the middle of winter Janae... *two* months."

"But...that's," Janae sputtered. "That's for work. Plus, I didn't *leave* the country. And you hate cruises! I thought you said you'd never get on one of those "diseased tin cans" as you called them."

"Well, I changed my mind. Look I didn't call to argue, just to let someone know I haven't been kidnapped and cut into little pieces."

"You mean not yet. Let me guess you want me to tell the rest of the family?"

"Nope, not their business, plus I know you are about to be buried with work. I just want you to stop them *if* they send the cops to break down my door. I dropped post cards off to my mama and daddy this morning. They should get them in a week or so."

"Okay fine. Text me if there's an emergency as I don't plan to check my email but once a week. When you said you didn't plan to do anything for your birthday you really just meant with the family, huh?"

"Something like that. I just wanted something different. Anyway, this line is finally moving. I love you! Hope you get everything you want accomplished."

"Love you too! Have fun, be safe and what the hell go with the flow! Happy early birthday!"

"Thanks! Gotta go, bye."

Hearing the dial tone Janae clicked off stunned. Shella was taking an international trip by herself. When had she even gotten a passport? Furthermore, Shella had one point in that her escapade was no weirder than Janae's. Guess everyone was trying new things for the New Year.

Janae didn't have much more time to think about it since the snow became heavier and dusk was creeping in. She *knew* she should have started out earlier, at this rate if she got in the house before sunset she would be lucky. Thankfully, her mid-sized SUV was able to manage the rest of the snow-filled drive and she ended up parking in front of the gorgeous two-story cabin around 4:45 p.m.

Struggling back into her coat, Janae zipped up then finally got out the car. Wasting no time heading to the back to get her bags. She had tried to pack light, considering. So she had one big case filled with clothes and miscellaneous daily things she would need. And a second medium suitcase filled with a few books she couldn't do without for referencing, her laptop, several notepads and a few more clothes. Quickly she went to the door and used the code Jonathan had given her, instead of the key that was buried in her purse. Dragging the two bags into the foyer, she immediately turned around and went back out.

Cold temps and insulated bags had allowed her to bring three bags of groceries from home. This should last her nearly two weeks if she didn't overeat from boredom. Which should *not* be a problem since she'd be working. Praying her inner threats would pay off, Janae placed the bags on the floor before locking the door.

Stomping the snow off her boots before pulling them off, she was excited to explore! Plus, the groceries would keep for a few more minutes. Slowly walking forward, she bypassed the kitchen unzipping her coat as she looked at the living room. This place was nice! She had seen the pictures online of course and knew it was modern and fairly upscale, still seeing it was believing. It made her self-imposed exile seem more bearable.

Everything was neat and tidy just as Jonathan promised, well except for one cup sitting on the large living room table, in the middle of the even larger sectional. All of which was in front of a gorgeous ash-stone fireplace. Other than that, not one thing seemed out of place. Heading up the stairs, Janae was interested in picking out a bedroom. She had gone back and forth between choosing one of the three larger rooms upstairs or the slightly smaller one on the main floor.

Crazy as it sounded, she worried about being on the lower floor in case of an intruder. She felt like being upstairs would give her more time to hear them and prepare to defend herself, on the other hand downstairs had access to the exits. Each room had a theme also, so she had decided to wait and take a look at each when she arrived. Not that it mattered about the décor, she should only be in there to sleep. She was here to focus, so help her God! If she kept reminding herself, maybe it would stick.

If memory served, the room to the right of the landing had dark navy and grays, which she had loved against the wood grain of the cabin. And it was the only room with a king size bed, not that she needed it. Easing the cracked door wider Janae peeked inside, happy to see it was just like the pictures. Well except for one thing, there was a half covered, bare-chested man in the bed.

Chapter One

Damond shifted, annoyed at that feeling of floating up to awareness. That in-between state of dreaming had him hearing a muted shrill voice. Which didn't make sense, he had been dreaming about riding on a speed boat with a party of half naked people. Seconds ago there had been hype and fun laughter around him, certainly not the panicky voice he was hearing now. Giving up the fight he scratched his chest blinking open his eyes. The action seemed to make his ears come fully online, though what he was seeing and hearing didn't make sense.

"I'm going to ask you one more time, who the hell are you?"

The voice was coming from a very pretty sista, who was wavering between enraged and fearful. Was he actually awake? He knew for damn sure he hadn't gone to sleep with a woman in the house, otherwise she'd be in bed with him. Sitting up he ran a hand over his face. When he looked over again the woman had an arm stretched out, pointing something at him.

"What the...lady if you use that pepper spray on me we're going to have a problem."

"We already have a problem! Who are you and why the hell are you in my house?"

"Your house? This is my place, the drain on my bank account proves it."

"Bull*shit.*"

The cuss word, in what until now was her slightly proper voice, had a grin splitting his lips. Which mystery lady didn't seem to appreciate, as her hand got a firmer grip on the small canister.

"Lady, stop pointing that at me and we can try to sort this out."

"There is nothing to sort out, you shouldn't be here. Jonathan loaned me the use of his place. *He* is an owner of the property."

Damond blinked hard, he hadn't had enough sleep for this shit.

"I'm aware that Jonathan, Dave, Kenneth and now *me* Damond Hall, are owners."

He watched as she finally lowered her arm and the expression on her face went from indignation to dismay.

"Look, let me get dressed and I can meet you downstairs and we can figure this out."

Miss Miffed just crossed her arms mental wheels turning, but the need to hit the can had him losing patience.

"You should take my suggestion to wait downstairs unless you want a free peep show. I'm getting out of bed whether you're here or not."

Not one to talk shit just for the hell of it, Damond reached for the end of the cover. Which caused the woman's eyes to widen in alarmed shock before she rushed out the door, slamming it as she went.

* * *

It took Damond about five minutes to use the bathroom, throw on some sweats and a sweater before heading down. Where he found the woman wrapping up a voicemail as she paced back and forth.

"Jon, please text me or give me a call back once you confirm who this man is." She looked directly at him before saying the next part. "And if he isn't legit please call the local police and send them this way."

Damond laughed, walking past her to the kitchen. He needed some coffee badly if he was going to deal with this testy intruder. He didn't bother turning around as she made her entrance.

"There has to be some mistake. You can't be here."

"And yet I am." She was a persistent little thing Damond thought, popping a k-cup in the Keurig before turning around. "You have me at a disadvantage. Who exactly are *you*?"

"I'm Professor Janae Williams, Ph.D. My colleague loaned this place to me for eight weeks. I even spoke to the property manager to schedule the time, her name was Amanda."

Janae held out her phone, where she had pulled up the confirmation email. The man barely glanced at it before turning to get his coffee. He still hadn't said anything, just took a few sips before she lost her patience.

"Now that we know that *I'm* supposed to be here, I'm sorry about any confusion on *your* part but you need to leave."

"Lady...Janae-"

"You can call me Ms. Williams." She stiffly corrected.

"Huh, you sure you don't want me to tack the Professor on, maybe the Ph.D.? Either way I have bad news for you. I'm not going anywhere...but you are free to leave. I'll even be a Good Samaritan and help you reload your car."

"But...but I have the email and proof! I scheduled this three months ago."

"I don't care what you have. For the record I do believe you. Once you said Amanda it made sense. I talked to her *four* months ago when I scheduled my time, she's a dingbat. The fact of the matter is I'm an owner and you're not. Plus I've been here a week already, and you just arrived. I'm here to finish my book and I can't have any distractions—so off you'll need to go."

The woman in front of him flinched back like his words had slapped her. When she suddenly glared at him and stepped closer, it helped squash the speck of pity that rose up in him for her situation.

"Look mister, I am not leaving. I have to finish *my* book. *I* just drove almost five hours to get here! It's not my fault the stupid lady *overlapped our bookings!*"

The livid professor had punctuated her last three words by poking him in the chest with her finger. Damond grabbed her hand in defense, he had felt those little sharp nails through his clothes.

"Do you think it's a good idea to put your hands on me lady?"

Janae snatched her wrist away as embarrassed color rose to her cheeks.

"I apologize, I was out of line. I'm just upset. This is very important to me, otherwise I wouldn't have put my life on hold to come up here."

"Look, I get it," he said mildly, looking out the kitchen window behind him. "You can stay for tonight since it's snowing. But I do expect you to be out of here come morning."

Janae straightened her already stiff back. Who did he think he was talking to?

"I don't care about your expectations. *My* expectations were to come here and write for eight weeks and it's exactly what I'm going to do."

"We'll see lady." Damond started walking away.

"My name is *Ms. Williams.*" Janae gritted out.

"Sure thing Professor. And try to keep it down out here, I'll be writing in my office."

Chapter Two

Janae barely restrained herself from slamming cabinet doors as she put the groceries away. She *so* wanted to be an asshole and make noise for the hell of it, but she wasn't unwise either. For now the stupid man had been pretty calm. For all she knew he could go from unbothered to outright violent in an instant. Done with the groceries she went to the bedroom on the ground level, thankful it was on the other side of the house from the office. Once inside she let go and banged everything she could, while putting up her clothes and getting organized.

Which bedroom she wanted was a moot point now. She wanted her sleeping quarters as far away from him as possible. Janae was finishing up around six when her phone rang. It was Jonathan with profuse apologies as he confirmed that Damond was the last owner who had bought into the property last spring. Reiterating the rest of them never used the place in the winter, which was why he'd suggested this time period to her in the first place.

She thanked him for getting back to her and told him it was fine, that she was sure the two of them could just share the space and hung up. For one brief moment earlier she had been tempted to use the presence of this man as an excuse to run home. But that was why she was taking this trip, to stop her procrastination on completing this project. Her lack of motivation, a first in her life at thirty-seven, was a real concern to her.

Was she burning out in her career already? Janae had compiled all her data almost a year ago, plenty of time to sort it out and write the book. Instead, she had been extremely lazy. Only getting two chapters of the book done before fizzling out. That's why she was going to stay *here*, no matter what annoying man she had to share the cabin with. After all, it wasn't like he could *make* her leave, could he?

What she'd seen of the man left no doubt he was strong enough to physically drag her from the house. She'd noticed once he was downstairs the man was at least 6'1 to her 5'6. And the bare deep brown chest she'd seen was solid and gently muscled. Janae could tell even dressed the rest of his body seemed to be in shape too. Conversely, he could simply call the police as she had threatened to do on him.

His face was good looking which in her mind made everything worse. A strong jawline framed his attractive lips, the same ones sending all the snide remarks her way. The thought of staying alone in a house with this fine brother made her nervous. Which was idiotic, since his looks should have no bearing on whether she felt comfortable. What should matter was that he was a total stranger and she was miles from anyone. But she could admit after the shock of seeing him in bed she'd felt a tingle of awareness, and when he grabbed her hand it triggered the feeling again. Attraction to the man already seemed to be messing up her focus, which she absolutely did not need.

Janae had been told that internet and cell service could be spotty, especially in bad weather. At the time it hadn't bothered her, figuring it would be less temptation to indulge in distractions from her work. Since the bulk of her research was done, there was no great need for internet anyway. The only thing that kept her from panicking and running out the door was that her family knew where she was. Jonathan had been told Damond was here *and* the man was listed as an owner and had apparently scheduled with the inept Amanda like she had.

So there was a mile long trail if he decided to kill her and dispose of the body in the woods. It wouldn't keep her from being dead, but at least her killer would get caught.

There was no sense in worrying about it now. Damond had rightfully pointed out that she wasn't going to be able to travel anywhere this evening. Janae could have made it to town and found a hotel *if* she had left at once, but now it was completely dark and the snow had piled up since she'd been here. Janae was stuck. Deciding she was finally hungry, Janae made her way to the kitchen to heat up a quick dinner. It had been one hell of a long day.

* * *

Damond had been writing for the last three and a half hours. Well if you could call writing a paragraph, followed by staring off in space for twenty minutes then repeating it all writing. He wanted to blame it on the surprise trespasser but couldn't exactly. He'd been here a week and for the most part it had been the same before the uptight professor arrived. Though her mere presence definitely wasn't helping his concentration.

He'd managed to get two and a half chapters done since he'd arrived on Christmas day. Though he cut himself a bit of slack since he'd also done a lot of in-depth outlining. The reality was he needed to quickly get his mind back on track and fingers flying across the keyboard. He was on a tight deadline, wanting to release a minimum of two books before the year was out, and was hoping to write a third.

Tommy, a close friend of his and a part-time writer, had listened to him complain about being in a writing slump, how he needed to put out more books before his fans lost interest. His boy had suggested he do a private writing retreat so that he could focus with no distractions. That's how his name had gotten passed along to Dave, the guy who let Tommy use his place once a couple years back.

Dave had been cool and the more they talked Damond shared that he took this craft seriously. At that point Dave suggested he buy into the timeshare. Their contract was set up for four people max and Dave was convinced this would be a great place for him to come once or even several times a year to hammer out some novels. At first he'd had doubts it would be worthwhile. But the more the man talked about how the other three rarely made use of it, Damond began to re-think the proposition.

Also Dave swore it was a quiet, private place year-round, yet very updated so it didn't have that *Misery* feel to it. A place away from the hustle and bustle of Southfield had sounded nice. His city had swelled in population in the last twenty odd years, which meant more people, restaurants, businesses and nightlife. So a place where it would be just him, a computer and nature might be the thing to jumpstart his imagination. Damond sorely needed something to work, since his creative ideas seemed to have taken a vacation from *him*.

So he had gotten out his checkbook which was wavering on the downside and took the plunge. Feeling oddly excited to turn into the trite "hermit" writer of movies, though he would prefer not to turn insane or any of that shit. The hope was to produce a lot of content at this place. They also had to be stories that would *sell* and fatten his pockets at the end of the day. What was great to a writer vs. a reader often didn't match up. Which was why he didn't need the added issue of Janae to deal with.

He could already tell the woman was going to be a problem. Most women would have run from the house as soon as they saw him. Instead she'd thought it prudent to stay, wake him up, *and* confront him. She was the exact type of character that would be killed off in his books. On top of it all, the woman had the nerve to be bossy, telling *him* he was leaving. As if she wasn't the one who just arrived. This woman was trouble.

Hell, she was probably crazy.

What woman would drive all the way to nowhere and spend eight damn weeks by herself in the winter? Damond was a night owl, and his creative juices flowed easier in the late evening and night than the daytime. He'd stayed up the night before until four a.m. and gotten up a bit after ten this morning. Which was why he'd been tired and taken a nap around three-thirty before being rudely awakened an hour later by Janae. Taken by surprise and still a bit sleepy he'd found the intruder amusing if slightly annoying at first. But the more he thought about it the more he was becoming irate.

This was supposed to be *his* writing haven away from people, noise, and damn sure from women. He didn't think it was a coincidence that his writing had dried up at the end of his relationship a year ago. Even before that, dealing with Veronica's drama and extreme need for attention had been a drain on his productivity. Damond had been sad to see her go, but not enough to even *try* getting her to stay.

Now the lovely if clueless Ms. Williams was determined to be a pain in his ass, he just knew it. As if he'd conjured her up she called out his name before a knock sounded at the door, opening a second later. Sighing, Damond swiveled around from the desk.

"You have a horrible habit of opening doors, I see."

"Sorry, when you didn't answer I didn't know if you were still in here or what."

Her voice didn't sound sorry to him, as she stepped inside leaving the door wide-open. Did she think he was going to ravish her and needed an escape route? Well at least she didn't have a weapon in her hand this time. Damond ran his eyes over her assessing. Out of the bulky winter coat he was able to get a better look.

She was about average height and a little slimmer than he preferred in her black loose-fit jeans and knitted green sweater. But she did have a handful of ass and chest for a man to grab, and really that was all you needed. Now her face was pretty as a picture. But her hair was pulled back into a low tight bun making her look serious, and making it hard for him to gage her age. Her lips were a nice natural shade and had some meat on them too. Normally, Janae was enough of a looker that she *should* be worried about him, but in this situation he wanted nothing to do with her.

"Well, as you see I'm still here. What do you want?"

"I just wanted to check in. I've settled into the bedroom down here and took myself on a little tour of the rest of the house. It's just as nice in person as all the photos."

"Yeah I like it, glad it's mine."

"*Anyway*. Just wanted you to know I'm turning in. It's been a long day."

"You do that, so you can be nice and fresh for the drive home tomorrow."

Janae ignored his pointed comment. Looked like the unconcerned man had turned testy. He might as well get used to it. They would be a thorn in each other's side.

"I do want to be *fresh*, so I can get to work on my research book. I never asked earlier but what type of book are you working on?"

"Understandable, as you were too busy threatening me with the police. I write murderous thrillers."

"Really..."

Her voice wasn't shocked nor interested, merely dry and dismissive. Which didn't surprise him. Many academic people were literary snobs when it came to fiction writing. Damond felt a smile returning to his face, as he stood and walked around the desk.

"You know, stalkers, psychos, characters who keep body parts as souvenirs." He had backed her out the door. "Folks who hold their victims captive in out of the way places, much like this one. Then leisurely have their way with them for days, months and in a few cases even years. Anyway, sleep well Professor."

Damond shut the door in her alarmed face. Let her think on that while she slept.

Chapter Three

When Janae woke up bright and early the next day the house was quiet. After making breakfast she decided to set up her work in the living room. It was almost noon before she heard any movement from upstairs, and another half an hour before he came down. Janae gave him a distracted greeting as she was reviewing her outline, and heard him grumble something back. She could feel him staring at her, but when she finally turned around he was gone. The man had proceeded to putter around in the kitchen for a while and then the office door shut hard. Four hours later he stomped upstairs.

They saw each other again around seven that night and she tried to be polite and was greeted with gruffness for her efforts. Figuring it was for the best, she parted from his abrasive presence as soon as possible. Glad that at least he wasn't trying to kick her out anymore. Janae could be reasonable and admit they both had cause to be annoyed. Besides she needed to be thinking about her own issues, like finishing this book.

This was her first solo work, but that wasn't enough to explain why she was so discombobulated. Her topic was on aggression in society through the lens of nature vs. nurture, nothing that hadn't been done before. Which meant there was plenty of source material she could look at, not to mention her own data. At the moment it just felt like her passion for the field of study had gone AWOL. Didn't she want to stay on track to reach tenure?

She could leave education and go strictly into research. Earlier in her career she had interviewed for a marketing company, but didn't feel right helping already rich companies take more of the American public's money. Had her goals changed? Janae enjoyed teaching at Eastern Michigan University. Expanding and helping to shape young minds, even as she struggled to hold their attention outside social media. The latter was changing her field of study drastically. Frankly, she and her colleagues were lagging behind in tracking and studying the effects of social media on behavior. But social media was like a genie in a bottle, you couldn't put it back in once it was out. In fact, that was going to be her next major research topic. Right now, she put the thought of where her career was going to the back of her mind, she had a book to piece together.

* * *

It was Saturday, the fourth day after her arrival and the best she could say was they hadn't murdered each other yet. Janae tried to focus but it was hard going, her notes and outline were pretty solid, but very little new progress had been made. She hadn't found a place in the house that seemed to get her energy flowing. Going as far as setting up her writing in different places, like the basement and the kitchen. She hadn't lasted more than a few hours in both.

Janae felt she would be better served writing in the office, as that had been her work space at home. But of course that space was taken...or was it? Maybe it was time she started using her expertise on her unwanted housemate. Shamefully, it was beginning to look like all her training went out the window when around Damond. Leaving her work, she padded down the hall in her sensible plain slippers, giving a little knock before opening the door.

"Hi, do you have a few minutes to talk?"

He was scribbling in a small notebook she had noticed once before. He didn't even look up at her entrance, but she noticed his forehead wrinkle and his mouth tighten.

"I asked if you-"

"I heard you the first time." Damond finished his last line and tossed the pocket-sized notebook on the desk. "Aren't you supposed to be some kind of psychologist?"

"How do you know that?" Janae asked startled.

"I know people too. My guy talked to *your* guy. So are you going to answer the question?"

"Yes, I'm a social psychologist. I study the behavior of people and groups including how people behave in social settings and how groups or individuals can influence behavior."

"Then you must suck at your job because your interpersonal skills and non-verbal cues are horrible"

"And you're a very rude man!" Was the best come back Janae had for that, particularly since she had just been thinking close to the same thing.

"Lady, you have a lot of nerve calling me rude when you just barged into my house, bedroom and now my office. You don't know what you could have walked in on."

"You know the bedroom thing was a mistake." Janae frowned. "And the only thing I expected to interrupt today was your writing."

Letting out a little amused laugh, she pointed at the bookcases around the room. "I mean there's not much else you could be doing in here...reading isn't scandalous."

"I could have been jacking off for all you know Professor."

Heat crawled across her skin, and her brain scrambled to make sense of his words. Damond's hand doing the up and down motion made her powers of deduction easier.

"Why...would you be doing that in the middle of working? You're just trying to be shocking."

"Why?" Damond let out a genuine laugh. "The why is simple—I'm a man. Two, it relieves stress and can get the creative juices flowing. Maybe you should give it a try."

"I don't appreciate you being deliberately crude, just to try and run me off." Janae crossed her arms, taking a step closer to the desk. "It's not going to work."

"You think too much of yourself." Standing he leaned forward. "I was being deliberately *honest* and making a point that you need to stop walking uninvited into rooms *I* occupy. Now, what exactly do you want?"

Janae swallowed the biting words racing up her throat and tried to focus on her goal.

"I apologize. We should be respectful of each other's personal space. On that note...I was coming to talk to you about our work areas. I'm having a hard time finding a place that seems to, as you said, 'get my creative juices flowing' and I was wondering-"

"Have you tried masturbating?" He asked seriously.

"That...is not an option I'm willing to consider," Janae said tightly.

"Suit yourself. What does your inability to write have to do with me?"

"I work in my office at home, so I was wondering if I could use this one."

"Hell no!"

"Come on! Why not, since you seem to be able to get your *juices* going wherever."

"Lady, why don't we all stop saying juices. It sounds really odd coming from you."

"You started it." Had she really just devolved into childish bickering? "Okay, can we at least share the space? Maybe I get the morning til early afternoon and you have the rest of the day?"

"No," Damond declared resolutely pointing to the cluttered desk. "As you can see, I have tons of notes laid out. I have no intention of packing up my stuff every day to make room for you."

She still didn't want to give up. "Well...what if I set up over on the sofa, maybe I can pull in a table-"

"No. First come, first serve. I have the office, deal with it. You have plenty of other options. There's a really good one if you don't like these accommodations...leave."

Janae sniffed, turned on her heel and didn't feel guilty for slamming the door on the way out. The man was insufferable. She always seemed to lose her footing when it came to him which just aggravated her more. If only he behaved like a civilized man, instead of throwing around masturbating like another person might say "I had eggs this morning". Maybe she would try one of the upstairs bedrooms for work, anything to stay away from him.

* * *

That's how she ended up co-opting one of the upper bedrooms that had good morning light as her makeshift office. Their different schedules contributed to keeping them out of each other's way. Which was why when she heard him jog upstairs a little after two, then stop outside her door, she became confused.

No knock came but she knew he hadn't moved on either. A full ten seconds later it was starting to freak her out that he was just standing there, when suddenly a hard knock came. Even though she was expecting it, she still jumped. Now *she* was considering whether to answer or not when he called out.

"Open up, or do I have to do one of your numbers?"

Being petty, Janae still took her time getting up and didn't answer.

"My bad," Damond yelled through the door again. "Maybe you finally took my advice and are getting yourself off."

"What do you want?" Janae flung the door open on a soft growl of irritation.

"Ahh, guess I was wrong, otherwise you'd be in a better mood," he teased.

"I'm busy. What can I help you with Mr. Hall?"

"I'm running into town to pick up groceries. Wanted to know if you needed to join me. *And* you can stop looking at me so suspiciously. I won't drop you off in the middle of nowhere and leave you…though it is a thought."

"Can you blame me? The thought of you doing a kind gesture puts me on alert."

"I don't know why, you still being here makes me the kindest man you know. I just figured it would make sense to do a supply run together, but it's up to you."

Janae thought about it, at least she wouldn't have to drive, and with being stuck in the cabin for almost two weeks she was itching to do more than just stand outside.

"Okay, I'd like to go. Thank you for thinking about me. When do you want to leave?"

"In fifteen minutes. I came up here to get dressed." Damond turned away, heading towards his room. "If you're coming, meet me downstairs by the door. If you're late I'll be leaving without you."

Chapter Four

Janae rushed to use the bathroom and get dressed for outdoors. It was cold of course, but hadn't snowed in the last few days at least. The blinding sun of winter was out in full force, so she had to shield her eyes while listening to Damond call her name and threaten to leave her from the other side of the door.

"What took you so long?" She quipped, not able to contain the snicker as he came out.

"Cute." Damond gave her a quick look over though he hadn't been talking about her outfit. "Come on, let's go."

The ride into town was going to take at least thirty minutes, and after a few minutes of silence Janae broke it with a question.

"I didn't ask before but where are we going?"

"There's a Meijer, figured we'd hit that since we can pick up food and anything else we need without running all over the place."

"Good thinking."

"Thanks Professor, does that mean I get an A in class?"

"Not yet, but we'll consider this your first paper and give you a B+."

"Damn, glad I never had you in college. Hated teachers like you. You have to basically give a pint of blood for a good grade."

"And I bet *you* were a joy for them too." Janae said dryly.

Pulling out a pad of sticky notes and a pen from her purse, she started writing as silence descended again. She was actually startled when he spoke.

"What are you writing over there?"

"Just finishing my shopping list."

Damond laughed and if it hadn't been at her expense she would have admitted it was a pleasant sound. His voice when relaxed was nice and smooth. Janae had the odd thought he could be a late night DJ by simply dropping his voice an octave. Yeah, like Keith Sweat and now she was the one chuckling.

"What's so funny?"

"Nothing, sorry I was just tickled. Keep your eyes on the road."

For the rest of the way they let the music fill the void. Strangely it was comfortable and by the time she hopped out the vehicle Janae was feeling fairly relaxed. Until they got inside and both tried to grab the same cart. For some reason she felt embarrassed as their hands overlapped. The thought of rolling through the store with a cart between them immediately made her think of an old married couple. Which was crazy since this task would be no more personal than the drive in was.

Clearing her throat, she spoke. "Uhh hmmm, do you want to meet here in say forty minutes?"

"That works but make it thirty, you have a list already."

"Fine whatever. These store layouts are basically the same no matter the location. See you then."

* * *

Damond didn't need all that time as he had his own mental list, but was trying to be considerate. Women and shopping in his experience never was a quick thing but maybe her list would help. Veronica his ex, had never used them, which always ended up with her complaining about something she'd forgotten. It had annoyed him to no end. Why was he thinking about his ex out the blue and Janae in the same context was weird because they were nothing alike.

Veronica had been impulsive, a very "living in the moment" type of person. Her body had been tall with ample curves, and he'd liked barely tilting his head down to kiss her. It was amusing but Janae was almost the exact opposite. He would stick a needle in his eye if coming up here to write wasn't the most "impulsive" thing that woman had done in the last five years.

The professor was slim, just above being skinny for her height, but she was shapely enough. Janae was short compared to the women he usually favored. Hell kissing her would give a man back pain without a doubt. Not that he wanted to kiss her buttoned-up behind. Still, overall he gave her props in how she had handled everything so far.

Most women would be whining about not getting their way, then again most women wouldn't have had the balls to stay alone with a strange man in the first place. She had some "grit" like his grandpa used to say. To be fair she mostly stayed out of his way, which was why he'd thrown her a bone with this shopping trip. Janae wasn't messy or extra loud or overly demanding, if you didn't count her trying to take his house and office. At that thought Damond chuckled loudly, causing the woman across the aisle to look at him strangely.

"Ballsy." He muttered, pushing his cart forward.

Janae had some nerve asking him to give up the office he'd claimed as his own, as if sharing his living space wasn't enough. He wondered had she gotten that stubbornness and never backing down from teaching the smart-mouthed and bold youth of today, or was it her natural personality? He figured it was probably fifty-fifty, or maybe she was just nutty. Turning his mind back to shopping he finished picking up the items he needed, all while remaining aware of the time. Refusing to let her accuse him of being tardy on his own self-imposed time limit.

*

Janae's list *did* help her with getting all the items she needed quickly. Like snagging some of her normal healthy items but also adding savory soups and pasta. The latter was usually restricted to eating no more than twice a month. Then she thought the hell with it and treated herself to some junk food too. Winter was a tough time as the cold meant less activity and the urge to eat a lot of fattening food overtook the mind.

One of those old ingrained habits in humans. The need to fatten up for the winter was imbedded in our DNA. That primal thought that food would soon be scarce as the cold came. At the core of it we were animals. Homo sapiens just got the luck of the draw, bigger brains and opposable thumbs is the only reason we were top of the food chain. Why look at Damond, some men were closer than others to their animal cousins.

Janae supposed she was being a little harsh. He wasn't a complete barbarian. She'd been holding her own against much more blatant assholes the whole of her academic career. Men who were snide just for the hell of it, like being snotty was a prerequisite to entering a Ph.D. program. Add in the misogynistic tendencies coupled with competition and you had grade-A bastards around you. Of course, this was a broad generalization. She had met and was still friends with a good number of perfectly nice male colleagues too.

No, Damond was just blunt, with a good dose of testosterone thrown in for good measure. He was similar to a few of her male students, a lot of barking and no bite. His sophomoric attempts to embarrass her with sexual banter also wasn't a first for her. Though she could honestly say no student or co-worker had ever made her blush from it. Then again, she'd never seen those people half naked either.

Damn it, why wasn't this line moving? And why did her mind keep going back to that image? Probably because it had been a year and ten months since she'd had sex. Her last foray at attempting to form a relationship had tanked five months ago and with it any hope her sex drive had or reigniting. Which she hadn't cared much about since "men and sex" fell into the larger category in her life marked *no time* and *often disappointing*. She chalked up her reaction to Damond as a by-product of visual stimulation and hormones. It would pass, besides there was no law against acknowledging a fine specimen of the species when one saw it.

Finally, it was her turn with the cashier and the subject was wiped from her mind. She was walking towards the door to wait when she saw him coming from the other direction. Janae would give the man his due, he was timely at least. Moving her cart out the way and waiting for him, she used the time to review the receipt for any mistakes.

"I think you're the first woman I've met who doesn't take all day in a store." Was his greeting as he parked alongside her.

"Do you practice being sexist or does it come naturally to you?"

"I like to believe all my talents are natural." Damond grinned unrepentant. "Let's head on back. Because you *were* on time, I'll ask if you feel the need to go anywhere else while we're in town."

"You are just a beacon of giving today aren't you? Thanks, but no. I'm all set."

"Are you sure," Damond pressed. "Because once I start the car the only direction I'm heading is to the cabin. I'm not coming back out again if you suddenly think of something."

"Okay." Janae frowned not understanding why he was harping on this. "Here's an FYI Damond, I'm capable of driving myself. Remember, *little ole me* drove all the way up here on her own." Her voice dripped with sweet condescending sarcasm.

"You're right...sorry about that."

For the first time she saw him look taken aback and he actually sounded contrite. They got the bags in the car after that, and as they buckled up she spoke.

"I did however really appreciate you bringing me along today, so thanks."

"No problem. I just didn't want to leave you at the house alone with my stuff."

That surprised a laugh from her, and it was a few seconds before she gave him a stern look.

"Trust me, you have nothing of interest for me to steal. Plus, I'm not a thief, just an unexpected house squatter."

Damond shook his head. Had she actually made a joke? Maybe Ms. Williams had a sense of humor after all.

"That's *one* thing we're in complete agreement about Professor."

They didn't talk much after that, letting the music do its thing again. His car must have satellite radio, because the R&B and Hip Hop couldn't be coming from a local station. When they arrived Damond parked, clicking open the hatch to the back before they got out. She took three of her bags and went to open the door, sitting them just inside, using the heaviest one to prop the door open. Then she went back to get the rest, passing Damond loaded down and coming her way.

"You didn't have to try and carry everything. I was coming back to help."

"I know and I didn't," he said. "There are still two more in the back."

"Oh...okay I'll get them."

And she did, snagging one in each hand before heading back. This time her head was down watching her step, as she had slid a little before. So when the cold projectile hit her squarely in the crook of her neck she jumped, dropping the low hanging bags. In shock, Janae looked up and over at the man already forming another snowball.

"Damond you've lost your damn mind!"

Leaving the groceries to fend for themselves, she ran back behind the car, buying some time to form her first missile. Peaking around the corner she saw Damond wasn't the waiting kind and had advanced forward. Doing the unexpected she jumped out and let him have it, hitting the top of his head before he could completely avoid it. A giggle escaped before it turned into a squeal as he let loose his own.

Janae ran, scooping snow as she went trying not to fall. The next hit landed on top of her head as it was lobbed over the car. Shrieking in outrage even as she busted out laughing. Instead of continuing around to the other side Janae waited for him to reach her. When he rounded the corner they both fired almost at the same time. Hers hit first throwing off his aim, and so it hit the back of her shoulder as she was turning to avoid it—and slipped.

Damond didn't think he'd hit her that hard, but Janae was laying on her face, not moving or saying anything. He went to check as maybe the fall had done some real damage.

Bending down he shook her. "Are you okay?"

Janae flipped grabbing his arm, pulling him off balance at the same time she rammed a handful of snow in his face. She fell back laughing like a loon as he landed next to her.

"Well played...you have a sneaky streak." Damond got out, catching his breath and rolling over towards her.

Janae's eyes were closed while she still laughed softly in the back of her throat. Like this, her face looked relaxed and happy, a change from all the severe looks he'd gotten since her arrival. Mouth stretched into a small smile, the color in her lips whether from the exertion or not, gave the impression of warmth. Damond didn't know what came over him, but he bent down intending to press his cold lips to her inviting ones. But when her eyes popped open, both of them stilled like deer caught in headlights.

"I think I dropped the eggs."

Chapter Five

After her inane comment they had gotten up, brushing off snow covered clothes before taking the last bags inside. Janae decided to attribute her increased heartbeat to the snowball fight, and *not* because she'd opened her eyes to see his handsome face above hers. So close she had seen the tinge of green around his brown eyes, and his kissable lips had been just inches from hers. Was it a wonder the stupidest thing ever had come out her mouth? Even so, once everything was in the kitchen she followed up on her hunch.

"Oh crap, I was right. I broke two eggs. Or rather *you* made me break them."

Damond looked over her shoulder at the damage. "Are you hungry?"

"Huh?"

"*Are you hungry,*" Damond said slowly, as if she was hard of hearing. "We could have breakfast for dinner. Use those eggs so they don't go to waste."

"That's actually a good idea!"

"Don't sound so shocked Professor every time I have one."

Janae ignored that. "Anyway...what else are we having?"

Damond held up the box of Eggos he'd bought and watched her mouth smirk.

"I guess I'll complete where this is going. I bought some small chicken cutlets so we can do the whole chicken and waffles thing."

Damond looked at the package on the counter and snorted. "What did you plan on using those little things for?"

"My salads at lunch, why?"

"No wonder you're so slim if that's how you eat." He ran his eyes up and down her body, snorted again and turned away.

"You're not going to shame me for eating healthy." Janae rolled her eyes. Until he started unpacking her junk food bag and just looked at her.

"Fine, I eat healthy "most" of the time." She said before snatching a bag of Cheetos.

"Whatever, *I'll* be frying up the chicken." Damond insisted.

*

Once the food was ready, they sat at the breakfast bar and dug in. Chicken and waffles, eggs, and toast. A bowl of cut fruit between them, and low and behold they had an actual conversation.

"What exactly are you working on up here?" Damond inquired.

"Well, I'm working on my first solo research book. Focusing on societal aggression when looking at nature vs. nurture. You know, how much environment plays into each person's level of aggression vs. societal shifts. And when a large shift happens to where violence or aggressive acts become the norm, who/what drives that?"

"That's interesting actually. If you figure it out I'm sure they'll give you a Noble Prize."

"You don't have to be sarcastic."

"I'm not, if you could figure out the why and the correlation that means someone could potentially figure out how to reduce it."

Janae sat up, surprised he was taking her work seriously at all.

"It's very complicated. Not one thing is a deciding factor for determining why individuals so easily follow trends, even violent ones. Then you have the inherited genetics to factor in as well."

"I didn't say it would be easy Professor. But just saying, if someone could figure it out I bet they would earn themselves some kudos."

"I guess you're right." Janae smiled ruefully. "But my hope for now is to understand it so we can get out in front of it."

"Got it. Want to know what I think?" Damond asked taking a long swig of the coffee he was having with dinner.

"I have a feeling you're going to tell me." She could see the tell-tale spark in his eyes that told her he was about to say something outrageous.

"People are assholes. It's that simple. People do what they think they can get away with. Whether taking a parking space that they clearly see someone is waiting on, or bashing someone in the head just to steal their Rolex."

"You really think it's that basic? I mean if that was the case all of society would be the Wild, Wild West."

"Don't forget, most of the world *was* for the longest, and to a degree still is. We had a need to work together through famine, natural disasters and the huge amount of predators that used to take us out. If not for that, we would never have thought about being *civilized*."

Janae thoughtfully chewed a piece of what she admitted was perfectly fried chicken, as she thought about his point.

"So you're saying you think that nurture, which evolved through species need, bravo for knowing that by the way, barely has a heavier influence over our natural instincts."

"Uh, yeah." Damond grunted. "I mean it took thousands of years to get to the point we are now. Yet, over 61,000 people die a violent death each year in the United States alone!"

"How do you know that?"

"Why would I not?" Damond grinned a little evilly. "You forget, it's *my* job to know about violence, murder especially Dr. Williams."

"Pick a name already for me. You're making me dizzy." Janae demanded, but it only made him grin harder.

"I don't think I will. Besides don't you know variety is the spice of life?"

"So they say. Tell me how many books have you published? Are you Indie or Trade?"

It was his turn to look impressed. "I'm surprised someone like you even knows about Indie publishing."

"Of course I do. Academics have been taking advantage of self-publishing in bigger numbers for a while now, even way back when it was expensive. If you had an ideal out in left field, you really had no choice since the university presses wouldn't take you. But now people do so fairly often. Probably for some of the same reasons it's so popular in the secular writing world. What little money we make from our books we can keep more of, as well as have more freedom with our ideas and subjects of study."

"You hit the main nails on the head, and yeah I'm Indie. For me it was because I didn't want to waste any more time trying to convince some agent to validate my stories worth. Plus, it's fairly quick, and as you said no editor having the final decision on what gets *in* my book and what doesn't. And last but in no way least, I want *all* my coins. Would you classify that as one of humanity's baser instincts...greed?"

"Yes I would, and I can't blame you there." Janae nodded across the table. "I've read a few articles over the years that say some Indie writers are making *big* money. Don't tell me you're some secret Stephen King who came up here to creepily write in the middle of nowhere."

"I wish." Damond let a wistful look claim his face before shaking it off. "I've got six books out that go a bit against the grain. I guess you can describe them as similar to "Dexter". They read from the perspective of the killer. You should study why so many people are interested in the minds of murderers."

Damond wiped his mouth and sat back before continuing.

"They were received well over the last five years. But part of why I'm up here is because I've been in a slight slump. If I don't pump out a book soon my readers may forget who I am. Indie is great, and I've been able to make an actual living off of it. But with so many writers in the market now, the competition for reader's short attention spans is harder than ever to keep."

"I'm sorry to hear about the slump." And she was, seeing as right now she could relate. "Looks like we came up here basically for the same reasons. Ironic, huh?"

"It's something alright. I think my problem is that I'm starting a new series, going the more traditional route, writing to trend. There will still be crazy killers but the books will focus on a law enforcement MC, oh that means main character."

"Thanks, I put two and two together."

"Well anyway, I'll be writing from a different viewpoint than I'm used to. With this being the first book, I have to put a lot of thought into the characters personality and how it will flow and even change in future books."

"I admit that seems more complex than I thought. I mean how far out ahead you have to plan. Good luck with getting your ideas together."

"Actually Professor, I just did." Damond pulled out his trusty notepad. "You just gave me an idea. I think I'm going to write in a psychologist to help out my MC from time to time."

"Me?" Janae watched him hurriedly scribbling down notes. "I mean not me, but I gave you that idea?"

"Yeah, it's not a new trope. Often there are partners trying to solve a crime or an outside co-partner of some kind. I just decided it would be amusing for my crime solver to bump heads with his own fictional doctor."

"Thanks, I think. To be fair you've given me something to think about as well."

"We'll there you go. We both have a new thread to pull on."

"Yes..." Janae trailed off, watching him pop a strawberry in his mouth.

Swallowing and turning back to her plate, Janae tried blocking the vision of his lips hovering over hers. Maybe he had never meant to kiss her. He could've just been seeing if she was okay. That was the more likely answer, obviously he found her too skinny for his liking, not that she cared.

"Umm, didn't you miss your nap today, are you going to make up for it now?"

Damond shook his head as he got up, taking his plate to the sink.

"No, it's too late for that. Besides, I want to outline this new character while it's fresh in my mind. Thanks again Professor."

And like that he was gone, his mind firmly on his work. Janae envied that focus and figured she needed to go find some of her own.

Chapter Six

It was Wednesday again and she had officially been here two weeks. Things were finally falling into place and she was making actual progress on her project. After their shopping trip and snowball fight, they settled into a kind of truce. Being more pleasant when they ran into each other, even falling into the habit of eating dinner together a bit after six-thirty each night. Whoever hit the kitchen first cooked, and by some unspoken means it was decided the other person cleaned up.

Janae thought it was fascinating to see communal cooperation happening in the moment between complete strangers. So of course she took a few notes for a future class, project or a possible research topic for her next book. It had been nice that the ice was finally broken. It also seemed to have been the catalyst she needed for her work to start flowing.

This particular day as they finished dinner she was thinking this getaway might end up working out despite how it started. She had been the one to cook, throwing together some spaghetti and meatballs, so there would be enough for tomorrow as well. Damond was wiping down the counter after loading the dishwasher when he suddenly turned around.

"Are you heading back to work?"

"Aren't you?" Janae questioned.

Normally Damond went back into his office while sometimes she would catch an hour of news on CNN or do her email check depending on the day of the week. Janae usually put in another couple of hours of work, then she was in bed most nights by ten. While Damond didn't turn in until around two-ish.

"No, I don't feel like it," he answered. "Plus, I have all night to put more words on the page. I was going to head downstairs, play around for a bit. Figured I'd give my brain a break. You should join me?"

Damond watched her mind work, and her eyes glance at the kitchen clock that showed it was already after seven.

"Never mind," Damond retracted. "I know you probably want to get more work in."

"No. I mean I do, but I can spare an hour of down time. Give me twenty minutes and I'll meet you down there."

"Yeah okay, no rush."

*

Janae didn't rush but she used her stated time to do her normal evening ritual. Damond had probably never noticed as he was closeted in his office, but she always went upstairs and put on bed clothes to get comfy before finishing her evening work. She took her showers in the morning, partly to help wake up. Unlike her unexpected roommate, who mainly wore sweatpants, she had packed as if she'd be running into people daily. Which in hindsight was stupid.

True her slacks were very comfortable, as well as the casual sweaters and shirts she had brought. But her Angelina Cozy fleece pj's were *beyond* compare when it came to comfort. Never had another pair been so super soft, yet still lightweight. They were keeping her nice and toasty at night too, she didn't even have to pile on the blankets. Shaking out her hair from its low bun, she tied on her headscarf before heading down.

In truth she was coming to depend on her brief but daily contact with Damond to keep cabin fever from setting in. Janae had thought she would relish not being around people, and in a way she did. No fake niceness to deal with from coworkers, no smart-ass kids that she wouldn't trust to vote on American Idol contestants, much less in politics giving her lip. Up here she didn't have to deal with the stress of traffic either. *Yet*, she missed it all, just a little.

Also, she wasn't spending her every waking hour working anyway. While being in the middle of nowhere allowed for less distractions, her modern human brain was in withdrawal from the lack of stimulation. Sure, she read a couple of chapters from the leisure book she had brought along, but that was about it. Unless you counted just staring out the window.

There were no sounds as background music for the ears, no people watching as you silently judged everyone. And at night no business or streetlights to prove you were not alone. The only thing out here that did that was Damond. All this left her with to much time for self-introspection, which was why no one had to twist her arm to take a break.

To date she hadn't spent much time in the basement, except that one time she tried to work there. The entire thing was one big game room to keep both adults and kids happy. She could see how this cabin would be a perfect vacation spot for a family. It ran almost the entire length of the house, except for a portion cut away for laundry, storage and the garage. The space had a pinball machine, pool table, ping pong, dart board even an arcade style two player basketball game. There was still room left over for a sectional in a seating area, and a rather large TV that was hooked up to a gaming system. Last, but always a sure thing was a card table in the corner along with a number of board games.

"I'm here."

Glancing over as she cleared the steps, his eyes widened. This was the first time he'd seen her in anything other than regular clothes, or her hair not in that boring bun. It was a shock seeing wavy dark brown hair hanging down her back.

"Hey, are you coming to relax or go to sleep?"

Janae flashed a quick grin. "Both, but some relaxing first. What do you have in mind?"

"How about some pool?"

"No, anything but. I somehow end up poking or hitting myself."

"I won't even ask how it's possible you can't avoid a big ole stick. You pick something then."

"How about basketball?"

"Sure thing, if you want to be assured of losing."

"I don't worry about things like that, I'm just trying to have a little fun."

She kept that mindset until they started to play, but once she made that first shot it became addictive. Her face screwed up in concentration as the minute timer counted down to zero.

"Damn Professor, you got a little game or I'm rusty. I only beat you by six."

"I don't know about that, I think it was luck on my part. Let's go again."

He beat her by even less the next time, though they both scored more overall on account of being warmed up. They played another two times and she actually won the last game.

"Okay, that's enough of this." Janae was breathless from the frantic throwing, not to mention the laughing and trash talking Damond had egged her into.

"Oh, now that you've won, you don't want a rematch?"

"It's not that, I'm just tired and want to do something else."

"Yeah right. Anyway, so you won't care if I pick what we do next?"

Janae nodded in agreement. "Anything but pool I'll give a try."

"You should know better than to tell a man *anything goes*. You know our nature means we'll try to take advantage of it."

Janae figured if her face was flushed she could blame it on the game. He had stopped trying to make her uncomfortable with sexual barbs after last weekend, so this one caught her off guard.

"I trust you not to be sadistic with your pick. Besides there's not much here for you to torture me with."

"I need to write you into a book, as the naive woman who gets killed in a creative way." Damond scoffed. "I'm sure I can find something down here to make you regret saying that. Just give me a few minutes."

"Have fun with that."

Janae went to the corner grabbing water from the mid-size fridge. Bringing one back to Damond as he fiddled with the TV. He took the beverage but gave her a funny look.

"They didn't have a beer or at least a coke?"

"They do, it's pretty well stocked. Drink the water, I never see you drink any."

"I wasn't aware you were monitoring my water intake."

"You can walk over and get something else, or tell me what we're about to do. My hour of downtime is ticking away."

"We're going to test your dancing skills." Damond rubbed his hands.

"What?" She almost dropped the water as he tossed her a controller. "Are you serious? I didn't take you for the kind of man to play this type of game."

Damond frowned. "What do you mean by that?"

"Just that you seem too manly to dance *dance*. You seem like the kind of guy that would sit in the corner of a nightclub, sipping a drink and looking out with disdain at the crowd."

"Oh really?" He didn't know whether to be offended or laugh. "Well, I can't see *you* in a club at all, so there. Do you even know how to move your hips?"

"Just pick a song with a decent tempo." Janae cocked her head, putting her hands on the very hips he was insulting. "And we'll see whose hips move better. You are *so* obnoxious."

"Careful Professor, I'm getting offended by your strong language."

"Shut up, and start the game."

Damond did, starting "Just Dance". Picking the first song "Finesse" by Bruno Mars and Cardi B. There would be no easing into it for either of them. With the songs up tempo 90's style it didn't take long before they were struggling to keep up, tripping over themselves and trying not to laugh, all at the same time. Somehow, they survived the almost four-minute long song without falling out, and had even gotten the hang of the routine somewhere along the way.

"Alright now! I see you Professor, you got some moves. How old are you? You were dancing like this was your era."

"Cause it is."

Janae paused for some water. That routine plus the b-ball undoubtedly equaled one of her rarely used workout tapes. This is what messing around with Damond got her.

"You didn't do so bad yourself. I'm thirty-seven, you?"

"Thirty-eight." He was thankful for that water now but wouldn't tell her that. "Hmm, okay you ready for the next one?"

"Sure why not, I've already embarrassed myself, what else do I have to lose?"

"There's always pride. One of those emotions that have people using violence to settle disputes. Later people slapped each other in the face with white gloves over it."

"You and all your annoying, yet accurate observations." It was such a male thing to say but he was right. "Maybe you should be the psychologist." Janae mumbled the last before saying louder, "Just start the next one."

Up next was "Mad Love" by Sean Paul & David Guetta featuring Becky G. A medium tempo song with a sensual Latin beat. They ended up doing some light salsa foot work, moving their hips was a must on this one, with some body rolls thrown in too. The movements were definitely sexy and before it was done she was feeling hot and bothered and not because of the activity. Watching his backside not to mention his front, left little to the imagination in those sweats. Both had her blood pressure going up.

When this song ended Damond gave her a long glance. "My bad, your hips move just fine Ms. Lady. I apologize."

"Are you sure that's water and not vodka because I can't believe you apologized about anything." Janae made a joke of it, because the way he was looking had her nervous. "I'll do one more song, but I'm picking it. You're trying to kill me."

Janae scrolled through the songs, finally choosing one pretty much at random.

"You really are trying to slow it up." Damond eyebrows rose as 'I Feel It Coming' by The Weekend queued up. "That's an unexpected choice."

"Honestly I only picked it because I've heard my students mention the artist before, I barely know any of these folks."

They got going and she quickly figured out what Damond meant. The beat might have been sweet and slow, but the words quickly got to her. Talk about "a single touch, seeing it in your eyes" started making her think thoughts best left in her subconscious. And when it started talking about "heat between your thighs" it was too much for her.

"I'm out, I'm tired."

Janae walked away not giving him time to protest. She made it to the area with the pool table and hopped on top. Head tilted back, her eyes closed while she fought to suppress her crazy thoughts. Time went by, maybe ten seconds maybe twenty, she didn't know. Just knew the music was still going when she finally lifted her head and opened her eyes, only to see Damond standing directly in front of her.

"Just a suggestion but the next time you try to escape, you should run further than across the room."

Janae licked her dry lips, nervous at his proximity and intense stare. "What in the world would I be running from?"

"Me."

Chapter Seven

Damond didn't give her time to speak, and neither of them much time to think as he caged her in with his body, leaning his head in for a kiss. *Just* slow enough so she could stop him if she really wanted to. When she didn't, he attacked her lips, slashing his against hers. Firmly demanding entrance, so that when her mouth finally opened she gave a little squeak of surprise. Only for them both to sigh a moment later when their tongues touched. Then he was putting his hands in her hair, not surprised it was as soft as he'd imagined it was.

For the first few seconds Janae held herself rock still. Everything but her tongue froze, as he invaded her mouth like a conquering Roman soldier. But when her shock wore off, she found herself leaning forward and grabbing his waist. He responded by walking even closer, nudging his hips between hers and that sensation alone through her pajama bottoms had her melting. Triggering her arms to wind around his neck, pulling him even closer if that was possible. The clothes were the only thing keeping him from being inside her and the thought had her gasping out in titillation.

Damond took the opening to run soft kisses down her neck to her collarbone. Only to trail his tongue back up until he could fasten his lips to hers again for an even deeper kiss. His hands were on their own mission sneaking under her top, walking up her ribcage until he could cup the undersides of her breasts. When she let out a little moan just from the light touch he determined he wanted to see what she sounded like when her bare flesh was in his hands. Pulling back, he whipped her shirt overhead, her glazed eyes sharpened as he went to get rid of her sports bra. Shit was she about to pump the breaks? Turned out she had just the opposite in mind, as she started pulling his own shirt off, and Damond was eager to comply.

Janae wanted to see and feel him too! Wanted to see that naked chest of his again, but this time really take it in. Her fingertips tingled as she started at his hips, sliding her hands up his stomach, circling his chest. Her eyes were locked on his smooth skin, though she could feel him staring at her face. Janae thought it was sweet how he was holding still like a patient animal trying not to scare another, but at this moment she wanted the heat and fire back. The embers of which she had been feeling since they started dancing.

Dragging her fingers through the small hairs between his pecs, Janae spread her fingers grazing his nipples. That seemed to get him moving. With the hand not supporting her back he tilted her head so their eyes met a moment before their lips did. And there it was, that fire again. It poured into her as he pressed their upper bodies together, and their skin connected. But she wanted even more, wrapping her legs around his bottom. Dragging, pulling him until she could feel the hard ridge of his dick.

Moaning Damond went to pull the sports bra down. "You distracted me." Kisses rained down her chest as he freed one breast. "From my original goal."

Damond had never been good at denying himself things, so he put that first sweet nipple in his mouth and pulled. What ensued was sexy little moans from her throat as his hips pumped against her sex. While he took his fill of both breasts, her legs climbed higher and higher on his waist, affording him the leverage he needed to slide her pants and panties down a bit. Enough to allow his searching hand to sneak between her legs, where he found her already wet. Sliding his fingers inside as he pulled her left nipple with his teeth.

"Damond!" Janae cried out, back arching like a drawn bow as pleasure shot through her system.

Then she was clutching his head to her chest with both hands, not wanting to let go of any of the pleasure he was giving her. Unfortunately, it tipped them both over a bit until she was lying flat on the pool table, their lips reaching for each other again, all while he fingered her to an orgasm that came out of left field. Her little scream of delight and completion was swallowed by his hungry mouth.

Suddenly he was gone, and she wanted to ask why but her voice was caught somewhere in her chest. Vaguely she felt him pulling her clothes from her body, sighing with relief when she felt him move between her lax legs again. But she wasn't prepared for the feel of his wet tongue against her extended clit.

"What...you can't-" Janae words died, her head snapping back as he sucked on her little bundle of nerves.

"Watch me," Damond demanded. "I want you to watch me. Raise that brilliant head of yours and watch me eat your delectable pussy."

Like a puppet on a string her head lifted, but her eyes struggled to focus. Only when they locked with his, did he slowly lower his face again, tongue first. He kept eye contact until his tongue curved to dip inside, then the delicious flavor that was her had his own eyes closing as a shiver of desire swept his own body. Once he had enough control he went back to his task, using his hands to spread her thighs wider so he could fuck her with his mouth.

He could have lapped at her forever, the taste and smell of her a drug for his senses. And every so often when he peeked up, the sight of those perky small breasts heaving, her eyes disorganized with ecstasy made his balls tighten each time.

When she showed signs of coming again, he made sure to watch it all. Rode it out with his tongue circling her clit until she was limp on the table. Damond gave her one last slow lick upwards, before lifting his head and swiping his tongue around the outside of his mouth, he wanted *every last* drop.

"Damn, we need a condom." Damon was almost as dazed as she was, as he looked around as if one would magically appear.

Janae was literally dizzy and she struggled to stutter out a reply. "I'm on birth control."

"I wouldn't have guessed you rolled like that." Damond chuckled, pushing his joggers and underwear down to his knees, more than ready to get down if she was. Still drunk on her nectar, he didn't immediately recognize the silence for what it was, a sign that shit had gone left.

Janae sat upright, his careless comment like a dash of cold water in her face. "What an ignorant thing to say! What are you even trying to imply with that statement?"

"You're right, it was an unneeded asshole comment, blame it on the situation. A lot of my brain power is below my waist right now. I should get a condom from my room regardless."

"Oh, *you* brought condoms to the middle of nowhere...*damn men.*" Janae grumbled, righting her sports bra at the same time reaching for her shirt. "Never mind, just hand me my damn pants."

Damond complied on auto pilot. See this is what sex did to a man, made him dumb as rocks. He realized it wasn't a good sign that she was getting dressed, and he didn't think telling her he'd picked up condoms on their store run would help. As he was registering the furious look on her face, he concluded it would probably get him a fist in the eye. Well with Janae more likely a stern talking to. Then again she'd surprised him tonight by almost letting him take her on a pool table, so a punch to the face might not be so farfetched.

He tried again. "Just so you know, I'm disease free if that's your worry."

"Do you think or do you know?" He went to open his mouth but she waved him quiet, jumping to the floor. "Doesn't matter, I'm not sure I'd believe you either way."

His annoyance was rising. "Why the hell would I even bring it up if I was lying?"

"I don't know, and it doesn't matter since *no one* is engaging in sex with or without a condom. My temporary insanity has passed."

Janae ran her hand over her head, noticing her scarf was missing. There was another in her room that would have to do, she just wanted to get out the basement at this point. Reaching the stairs, she went up a couple before turning to address him again.

"Look, this...was unexpected so let's just forget about it. After all it's not going to happen again.

"Why the hell not?"

"Because neither of us have time for this, we both need to focus. Let's go back to co-existing. Roommates, ships passing in the night."

Damond just looked at her, hands on his hips. His inflated cock still slow to get the message that it wasn't happening tonight. This woman was crazy! They'd just had excellent foreplay and she was talking about fucking ships. But she did have one thing right, sex with her uptight behind would be complicated. His focus was already messed up by her mere presence.

"Yeah, sure whatever you say Professor."

She thinned her lips at the nickname but continued up the stairs. "Good night Damond."

* * *

Apparently Damond had taken her flippant comment about being ships passing in the night to heart. Over the next five days they were rarely in the same room. If it wasn't for the occasional noise she wouldn't think they were in the same house. She had been stupid spreading her legs for that man, it *must* have been cabin fever. She wasn't sure how else to explain it as she sat in her makeshift office. If she were being honest, it had been so long since a man touched her, that she probably would have gotten aroused by anyone. But was that really true?

Janae doubted she would have let just *anyone* kiss her much less tongue down her lady flower. Damnit, she hated when her inner dialogue sounded like a seventy-year old southern belle. Great, she was rambling in her own head, which meant she was stressed and unfocused. Pushing back her laptop in disgust, Janae rose from the dressing table/desk and laid down. She had been without a man's caress, the feel of their larger rougher hands stroking her flesh for a long, long time.

"Damn him!"

The man had her mind going to places she had dug a deep hole, buried those feelings, and put a slab of cement over it. Just the thought of how his hands and tongue played her body *just right* had her squirming and her own hand trailing down to massage her center. The resulting flash of pleasure snapped her to awareness, made her remove the naughty hand like her pants were on fire.

Rolling off the bed Janae went to the window, staring at the falling snow while she allowed her body to cool down. She was determined not to give him the satisfaction of causing her to masturbate. Though as she sat back down to work, she couldn't wrap her brain around how denying *herself* was hurting him at all.

Chapter Eight

Damond couldn't lie, he was still pissed, not to mention confused from what nearly happened in that basement. The damn woman had left him with his dick hanging out, *literally*. Once he had pulled up his pants he'd powered everything down, including his desire, and headed up to his office. Figuring now was the perfect time to get his frustration out by writing a killing scene in the book.

Avoiding her in the days since, Damond didn't know if he was doing it as the best course of action or so he didn't lose his cool and go off. Was he annoyed he hadn't gotten any, *yes*! Shit, it wasn't like he'd asked her down to the basement with the goal of seducing her. They had been getting along with each other for a while and he just wanted to have some fun for the night.

Okay yeah, he'd picked up the condoms at the store, but that was just an instinctive male response. He was alone with an attractive and available woman. To the little brain in his pants that meant there was "some" chance he might get sex. Didn't matter if it was .05% or not. So he had prepared for the vaguest of possibilities, not really thinking he'd get to use them.

That damn snowball fight put the ideal of kissing her in his head, and he hadn't been able to shake it. Then it bubbled up again with all that dancing. His ploy to make her uncomfortable had ended with him being tortured.

Now he could distract himself well enough during the day by focusing on work, but at night he was left with a hard cock and a tired wrist. Lately he'd switched it up, and if this kept up much longer both hands would be useless.

So yeah, he was left feeling grumpy and figured laying eyes on her would make everything worse. Just like today, a couple of hours after skirting around each other at dinnertime he found himself back in his office gazing out the window. Snow had fell leisurely to the ground much of the day, but now it was coming down in sleets. The wind picking up so much the windows rattled. Startled by a streak of lightning, he stepped back. Damn, that was rare to see during a snowstorm. When it struck again the lights went out.

"Well shit."

Damond stood up, the glow from his laptop helping as he went to the bookcase for the flashlight stored there. He could already here Janae's footsteps scrambling above. Less than thirty seconds after the lights winked out he heard her coming down and calling his name. Sighing and wishing he had a drink he went into the hall, meeting her at the bottom of the steps.

"I'm right here Janae."

"Thank God. Did you see that lightning? I can't believe the lights went out, this is creepy."

She was rambling and Damond was surprised to see her so freaked out over a little power outage.

"Relax Professor, I'm sure the lights will be back soon."

"How do you know?"

Janae hated the panicky sound creeping into her voice, but she absolutely *hated* the thought of being in the dark while here. Once night hit in these woods it was pitch black, now with the lights out it was suffocating. Lifting the battery-operated lantern she had found in the corner upstairs, she moved into the living room.

"Because they went out the first week I was here," Damond answered her question trailing behind her.

"How long did they stay out?"

"I don't know, it was right when I was taking my nap. All I know is that they were back on when I woke up two hours later."

"Great, so you have no clue. It could have been the generator kicking on for all you know. You sleep like the dead."

Damond shrugged. "I guess."

"Speaking of, why hasn't the generator come on? When I was looking into this place it said there was one for times just like this."

"Yeah there's one, on the side of the garage."

"Why hasn't it popped on?" Janae persisted.

"Have some patience, it's only been a few minutes."

"No, it's been closer to *five* minutes, generators are supposed to come on almost immediately."

"You know this because you have one at your house?"

"No...that's just the way it works. It's the whole point of having them, so you don't go prolonged periods of time without electricity."

"I don't consider five minutes to be that prolonged." Damond said dryly, only to have her whip around and glare at him.

"This isn't funny. You should go check on it."

Crossing his arms, he let the beam from his flashlight glint against the wall.

"I'm not laughing. Let me get this straight, you want me to go outside in over a foot of snow, to check on something you barely gave five minutes to work? Plus, the lights might come back on their own soon."

"Maybe, or maybe they won't for hours. I don't want to wait that long." Janae walked forward touching his arm. "Please, will you go see if you can get the generator working?"

Fuck, Damond felt mentally pushed into a corner. Did he ignore the pleading in her big eyes and become the biggest jackass in history, or did he become the biggest fool by trekking outside in the cold, snow and wind? All because she was afraid of the dark. Nature wasn't fair, some primal mechanism made men susceptible to big eyes *and* big asses. Both of which always spelled trouble.

"I'll go take a look. Let me get my gear on."

"Thank you!"

When he filed out to the hall she was right on his heels. He ignored her, putting on his parka, hat and struggling into his boots. Opening the door the wind hit him hard. Damond glared at her, only getting a tepid smile in return.

"I *really* appreciate this."

"Yeah, yeah." He took his flashlight and headed out.

He had only gone a few steps before he was cursing under his breath. The wind whipping against his face felt like little needles. Picking up the pace as much as he could in the tall snow, Damond reached the side of the garage where the generator was housed.

Even before he shined his light on it, he definitely didn't hear it doing anything. Great, now to figure out why. Bending down he dug and brushed the snow from the small space separating the machine from the house. Once he got down far enough he saw the gen-cord wasn't attached to the transfer switch. He got a little pissed, and put it on the list of things to complain about to that horrible property manager Amanda. They were supposed to do basic stocking and a full check of the house anytime there was a reservation. Though he supposed it could have been knocked loose somehow, either way it wasn't hooked up.

Reaching out to rectify this he paused, drawing his hand back. Janae had been on his ass trying to be close to him with the lights off. If they stayed that way there was a good chance she would be forced to spend time with him. He didn't know if he wanted to do this to needle her a little bit, or because he wanted a chance to pick up where they'd left off. The little devil on his shoulder whispered it was probably both. It certainly wasn't the gentlemanly thing to do, but a case of simmering lust could make a man act out of character. Standing, he started walking back to the house, telling himself he wasn't being *that* much of a prick. Technically the lights could pop back on at any moment.

*

Locking the door after it closed, Janae's imagination would give Damond's books a run for their money right now. Because she was thinking a murderer who not only was a psycho but also a racist, had picked their cabin in particular for tonight's kill. They had disabled the generator to have more time to stalk and terrorize the victims of the house. She had zero logical reason to think any of this, but she 100% did.

While those "cozy" thoughts ran through her head she went around the house and found some candles that she had noticed before. Lighting one for the kitchen and placing two in the living room. If memory served there were more of the lanterns in the basement but there was no way she was going down there alone. She did tiptoe to her bedroom and get the pepper-spray from her keychain *just* to be on the safe side.

It seemed like it took forever before the front door creaking open startled her to her feet. As she hurried to the hallway, all she could hear was Damond cursing and stomping the snow off. What she wanted to hear was the whirl of a machine working or bright light stinging her eyes.

"What's wrong with it? You couldn't get it to work?"

"Umm no, and I'm not sure why." He preempted.

"Darn it, what do you mean? Was it broke?"

"Look lady, I don't know. I'm a writer not a handyman. It's dark as shit out there. From what I could see there was nothing wrong with it, it's just not working."

"Well take me to it. Maybe I can figure it out."

"You're certifiable if you think I'm about to go out there again. It's still storming if you haven't noticed. Feel free to go by your lonesome."

"I just don't like being in this dark."

She sounded so dejected he almost felt bad for her. "I see you found some candles, so we're not in the dark. Let's get a snack, it'll take your mind off everything."

"Doubtful, but okay."

Janae sat on a stool in the kitchen, her lantern adding more light to the room, while Damond rummaged around.

"The Keurig probably still has hot water, you want some tea or hot chocolate?"

"I want some lights," she said peevishly.

"Well, that's not an option. And since you waited too long I'll pick for you, coco it is." Damond decided getting two cups ready as he got the mix down.

"I want marshmallows then."

"What did you say? Stop mumbling. I'm sure you don't encourage that in your class."

"You can be so annoying!" She snapped. "Did you hear that?"

Janae jumped up getting the marshmallows herself, popping a few in each cup before he added the water straight from the still hot tank. While he finished getting those ready, she opened her unofficial junk food cabinet. Grabbing a half-eaten bag of Oreo cookies.

"Grab my flashlight will you, my hands are full," Damond asked her. "Let's go into the living room."

Chapter Nine

Janae grabbed his light along with hers before following as they moved into the other room, where he set the hot beverages on the low table.

"I think I caught a chill out there, I'm going to start a fire. Plus, it will keep us warm and provide you more of the precious light you desire."

"That's actually a great idea, thanks."

She watched as he threw in a few fake fire logs to quickly get it going and then topped it off with a few of the real wood chunks that were stacked in the corner of the room. When he sat down on the bear skin rug next to her, she handed him his beverage.

"Thanks."

"No, thank you. I really appreciate you checking."

"Yeah, well you're welcome. Sorry I didn't have better results for you."

"No, *I'm* sorry for freaking out on you." She held out her snack as a peace offering.

"I get it, some people are afraid of storms." Damond took a handful of cookies. Figured eating would take away the sliver of guilt trying to creep in. "That lightning *was* freaky, even to me."

"I usually like storms, lightning and all *if* I'm in the house. They can be oddly relaxing. Ann Arbor weather is horrible. We're often hit harder than cities east of us, so I'm used to having no power for a bit."

"Then why in the hell was I outside in the dark if this isn't a big deal?"

"It's this place! At home I still have noise. Some stores and houses have generators so it's never *completely* dark or silent. I can't help it. I keep thinking about axe-murderers creeping around out there."

Damond chuckled. "The only murderers around here are in my books."

"That's all good and well, as long as they stay in there."

They sat in companionable silence for a long while after that last exchange. Finishing off their drinks and the bag of miniature Oreos as they sat. Janae felt more relaxed. The warmth of the flames and the glow it gave, putting her at ease. Right up until Damond blurted out the unexpected.

"So...be honest. You've probably gotten yourself off since the basement, right?"

"What?" Good thing she wasn't still eating because she would have choked. "I have not!"

"You don't have to lie. It's no big deal, it's natural to do it every once in a while."

"While that may be true, *I* haven't done it. Not that it's any of your business. I mean...maybe I thought about it once or twice since then, but that's it."

Why had she told him that? Better yet, why did she allow him to draw her into these inappropriate conversations? Looking anywhere but at him, she played lightly with the thin gold bracelet on her wrist.

"Nothing to be embarrassed about Professor. My once a day has doubled since our basement fun and I'm not ashamed to say it."

"You should be, where is your verbal filter? I don't want to hear about you diddling your fiddle while thinking of me."

Damond laughed so hard he leaned back on his elbows.

"Where do you get these old-timey phrases from? And your ego is a bit big. I said I was whacking off more, not that I was thinking of you while doing it."

"My ego has nothing to do with it, you brought up the basement so I assumed...ugh never mind. You are an aggravating man. Why can't you just sit here and be quiet while we wait on the lights."

He sat back up, even scooted a bit closer as she watched him warily. "But what fun would that be?"

"Everything doesn't have to be fun," Janae insisted. "Fun is what got us in a sticky situation last time."

"I disagree. Everything doesn't have to be *so serious* either. The lights are off, we can either work until our laptops die out or relax."

"Damond I *could* relax, if you would just—be—quiet."

He was for a while, shrugging before looking off into the fire, even throwing another log in it after a bit. But of course his silence didn't last long, it wasn't even a full ten minutes later before he was speaking again.

"I propose we pass the time by fooling around."

"The dark is making you delusional." Janae rolled her eyes, snorting out a laugh. "But feel free to find a corner and take care of yourself if it'll make you happy."

"Why play with myself when we can play with each other? You know one of the things that distinguishes higher level mammals is that they have sex for pleasure, not just procreation."

"*Another* trait which puts humans above animals is *not* being ruled by their sexual instincts." Janae shot back.

"Yeah, there's that pesky civilization making us boring again." Damond leaned in, crowding her space until she had to meet his eyes. "Why can't we do a little hanky-panky to pass the time? See I even used an old word...just for you."

Janae wanted to laugh but bit her lip not wanting to encourage him. "Get away from me with your dirty mind."

Damond didn't move, he saw the laughter in her eyes and knew he could get away with a kiss, and then that would be all she wrote. Truth be told half of him was trying to keep her mind off the dark, and the other part, one he didn't want to examine too closely, wanted *her* to come to him. Needed her to make the first move, so he not only backed away but got to his feet.

"Fine, I'll be in my office."

"Wait, what?" Janae quickly reached out, grabbing the bottom of his pants. "You're just going to leave me here alone in the dark?"

"I was doing what you told me. Figure out what you want Professor."

"I want *you* to sit down, stop teasing me and above all else don't leave me in the dark in this creepy ass cabin!"

"Language," Damond admonished, dropping back down next to her. "And for the record if you'd let me truly *tease* you, you wouldn't be so stressed about the dark."

"Whatever." She got out on a sigh of relief.

"Easy for you to say. I could have been spanking my monkey before having a nice nap instead of sitting here with you."

"You won't die if you don't masturbate. I've never seen a grown man be so sexually... needy."

Now Damond gave her a serious look.

"Then you haven't been around many *real* men. We're always looking for an opportunity, particularly when we're around a sexy woman. That's just our nature. Don't blame me for having actual testosterone. What do they do, neuter the men in academia?"

Janae opened her mouth, only to snap it shut and turn her head away. Damond was arrogant, aggressive with his words, and even pushy at times. He was very much a *man*. Despite what he thought, she was a normal woman and his sexual innuendoes were affecting her. Making her mind flashback to the basement interlude where he'd brought her pleasure, both with his hand and head between her legs. When she looked back around it was to find him still gazing at her. In a voice just short of a whisper Janae made an offer.

"I...can give you a handjob."

"You can do what now?" He had been expecting a number of things but none of them had been that.

"You heard me. Do you want one...I won't offer again."

"I'm wondering why you're offering now?" Damond was truly stunned.

"Why do you care? Didn't you just say men were always looking for an opportunity? Well here's one, do you want it or not?"

"Hell yeah I do. But I still want to know how *your mind* decided to offer."

Janae sighed, wishing she had kept the compromise to herself.

"That night you made me feel really good, and it's been a long time since I felt that way...sexually." She explained. "I also realize you didn't get to completion. I'm willing to pay you back so we can be even, and you can let this sexual tension you have with me go."

Damond bit the inside of his jaw so he wouldn't say anything rash. Like psychoanalyze her comment and point out how the sexual tension was mutual. But he had no desire to delay the outcome of what he'd been aiming for. Which was to get his hands on her again. True, for now it would be her hands on *him*, but he would take it.

"Okay, how do you want me?"

"Oh." Janae expected him to pick at her comments more as he was normally prone to do. "Just lay down. And to be clear, everyone's clothes will be staying on and *you* keep your hands to yourself."

"I know you're the teacher and all, but when you said handjob I was expecting the adult version." Damond put a throw pillow under his head and got comfortable. "You know hand to skin contact. Not the seventh grade version through my pants."

"I can get to your...where I need to be without taking off your clothes. Just lay there and hush."

Not giving herself time to change her mind, Janae proved her point by easily pulling down his joggers. His underwear took a little more effort as he was already half erect, but when he lifted his hips, she was able to pull them down far enough to expose his manhood. She had to take a deep breath at what she saw. In the basement by the time his pants were down she'd been pissed off, purposely looking anywhere except below his waist.

But now, she could see him clearly in the warm light and she was impressed. He was thick, growing even more under her curious gaze. When he cleared his throat, she finally touched his smooth flesh. He was warmer than her hand was, as she slowly started to stroke him up and down. By the time he was fully hard, which didn't take long, Damond was talking again.

"If I would have known you'd be handing out handjobs I would have brought some lotion."

"If you don't like it, I can stop."

"No, no, it's fine. You have really soft hands actually. They're a little sweaty so that adds some lubrication."

"Oh my God, would you please shut up!"

Janae stifled her laugh and refused to look at him, besides she was fixated with watching his penis. He felt huge in her hand and her mind couldn't help wonder what he would feel like moving inside her. Was she breathing a bit fast, probably but she couldn't help it. Barely two minutes later, he was bothering her again.

"Let me know if you need more light. I can do an "X" marks the spot with my flashlight."

"I've never met a man that talked so much who wasn't giving a lecture." She scolded. "What will it take to shut you up?"

"Well, if you tighten up your hand a little and move a bit faster for about three more minutes, I won't be able to. You know, because I'll be coming."

"You're so crass!"

Janae did what she should have done a long time ago. What she'd wanted to do since first touching him, shut him up with a kiss. Time froze as an electric shock went through them both. Then his hand was on the back of her neck taking over, barely before she began.

Janae didn't mind, she delighted in him taking control as he rose up, at the same time drawing her down with his other arm. His tongue probing every corner of her mouth, hers trying to do the same to his. They both tasted of sweetness and chocolate and it only made her want more. When she pressed even closer he let out an uncomfortable groan, because she was squeezing him. Loosening her grip she started stroking him again, so that the next moan he emitted was deep with fervor. Which had Janae smiling against his mouth, and Damond rewarding her with a nip of her bottom lip.

Then he was moving his hips, pumping into her fist as their kiss grew heated and frantic again. The hand on her back moved to deftly work her bun loose, the other thumbing her nipple while she lay half over him. When her own thumb stroked over the head of his penis an entire shiver racked his body. She heard him whisper, "damnit Janae" before he pulled away. The disconnection allowed the crackle from the fire to breach her ears, along with their labored breathing. Sneaking a look, she saw his face was relaxed as if the smoldering kiss hadn't tugged at his sexual appetite at all.

"It's getting late and not much we can do until the lights come back on. Which could happen soon or not."

Damond said untangling from her, even as his brain shouted for him to do anything but. He wanted her underneath him, while he took her in every way possible. But instead he tucked his penis away and righted his pants, as the exact opposite came out of his mouth.

"I'm going to head on up and take advantage of some extra sleep."

"Oh." Her brain was thrown off by this sudden turn of events. "You'll be able to sleep knowing the lights are out? I know I won't. I was hoping we could...just stay down here together."

"I don't think so. You know how I like my sleep, *in* my own bed. If you're really that afraid you can bunk in my room."

"Do you only have sleep on your mind Damond after that kiss we just shared?"

Janae was just as surprised at her bold question as his face showed he was. But he recovered quickly, only giving a small shake of his head before standing.

"Look Professor, I can accommodate either of your needs. A sleep buddy to ward off the scary dark or a fuck buddy to make you forget what day it is, much less the lack of light. But going forward they'll be no more of these college level sexual games. You need to be very clear on what you want and *don't* want from me."

Damond watched her eyes widen before lowering, color infusing her face. He'd been super blunt because he didn't want any confusion this time around.

"It's up to you, but either one will be done from *my* bed because that's where *I'm* going. Don't forget to extinguish the candles whenever you call it a night."

Chapter Ten

Acknowledging to herself that anything might pop out her mouth in that moment, Janae bit her tongue and only nodded as Damond headed upstairs. Staying in front of the fire with her arms wrapped around her knees, she watched the flames flicker in the hearth. Looking on as the shadows arched cross the walls of the cabin, while her brain thought in overdrive. Honestly, she didn't know which notion freaked her out more, sleeping downstairs alone or having sex with Damond.

She knew on her end if she shared his bed it wouldn't be to cuddle. And despite the restraint shown tonight she didn't trust him either. So it really all rested on what she wanted. Janae listened as he moved around above. To the toilet flushing, the shower running and the floor giving an occasional squeak as he walked over it. Another few minutes passed before she finally got up, grabbed her light and pinched out the candles in both the living room and kitchen.

Janae took a rare night shower hoping to sooth her nerves and stop her brain from going around and round in circles. After all, she knew there was only one option. The one that made sense, to focus on why she was here. Fooling around with a stubborn, sexy man who was too brash for his own good was *not* part of her plan. She barely had over four weeks to go and a boatload of work to do. Sex with Damond Hall was not included on her list of things to accomplish.

Janae didn't believe Damond was the kind of person looking for a relationship, hell, for that matter neither was she. It wasn't the right time in her life to be distracted by a devilish smile and an enticing penis. Besides, he would be the last type of man she'd choose for anything serious. The more she thought about it, the clearer her choice became.

*

It would be a lie to say he was asleep, when in fact he could admit his ears had strained to hear any sounds of Janae moving around downstairs. To be fair he did *try* to drift off, but that was a no-go, and he started calculating the odds she'd go for either offer. Though he could imagine she tried to be quiet, he heard the creak of the third step before the landing, as she came up well over forty minutes later. Janae was coming to him *or* a bedroom located upstairs at least. When the knock came at his door, he let out the breath he was holding. Jesus give him strength if all she wanted was a human body pillow.

Keeping his hands behind his head Damond answered, "Come in."

The door opened slowly and she eased inside. Since Damond had hoped she would come, there was one small candle lit on the bedside table near the door, and a lantern turned down very low on the other. More than enough light to see she was in a thick, floor-length plush robe tied tight at the waist. Damond decided not to waste time and got right to the point.

"What's it going to be Janae?"

She should run. Which was what she should have done the first time she saw him laying naked in this bed. But just like before she was glued to the floor. She must be out of her damn mind.

"I was hoping..." Janae unknotted the belt. "That it could be both."

As it fell from her shoulders Damond watched her bare dusky skin be revealed. Like a puppet on a string he sprung up to his elbows for a better look. Could she hear how his heart was pounding in his chest at the sight of her little round breasts, the slope of her stomach and hips? She *had* to hear it. Unless her ears were clogged with the sound of her own heartbeat. He could clearly see the nerves, behind the excitement in her eyes.

Twisting around, he opened the top drawer, turning back with a condom between his fingers. He saw her swallow hard then nod, before he let it drop between the pillows. Tossing back the covers so she could verify he was naked *and* quickly rising to the occasion, Damond quietly spoke.

"Come here."

It was all he could manage out his tight throat, watching every move of her body as she walked to the bed. As soon as she put one knee on the mattress, Damond snatched her close in an iron grip. Then did what he'd wanted to do downstairs, got her body under his, wedging his hips between her legs. Pressing her down into the mattress as her hands clutched at his back, his lips at her throat, then her neck and finally devouring her mouth.

If they thought the kiss downstairs had been a one off, that hypothesis was blown to shreds as the passion from before exploded again. *God,* her skin was so damn soft. The scent of her soap and her body's desire literally made his mouth water. Pulling on some depth of will power he didn't realize he possessed, Damond tried to slow it down, for her sake or his he couldn't say.

Trailing his lips to her jaw and cheek, Damond ran his hands along one curved hip, squeezing and shaping her thigh. While her hands made a path over his chest and shoulders, making his muscles clench and skin heat. He wanted this to be worth the bravery she'd shown in coming to him. Refused to let her leave his bed with any cause to regret the night. He already knew it would be exceptional for *him*, the goal was to make sure it was the same for her.

"Let me show you how hot you make me." He whispered, nipping her shoulder gently.

Janae nodded mutely, no clue what that meant or what she was agreeing to. As long as it was coming from him she would take it. When he reached across her picking up the small votive candle, she had no clue what he was up to. Until he sat up locking eyes with her and tilted it. The squeak of surprise was more from the act itself than any pain the wax caused.

The semi-liquid felt super warm as it splashed onto the meaty part of her breast. The first drop was barely firming when the second came down on the opposite side, making her gasp again. Her skin tingled and the slight sting combined with the cold air of the room caused her nipples to harden quickly. Janae was processing that sensation before he added another, suckling the hard tip into his slick mouth.

"Ooohh, Damond!"

He took his time, squeezing firmly to take even more in his mouth. Janae's body squirmed under his with arousal, and no relief. As if he knew her torment Damond shifted, placing one leg high in-between her thighs, while rubbing his extended shaft against the side of her body. Then he was repeating the wax process on the other breast, while she humped his knee against her swollen clit. All while he licked, sucked and kneaded her now sensitive breasts. Before long she was coming, writhing against him.

"You drive me crazy!" She panted out.

"No more than what you do to me."

Damond wanted the use both hands but wasn't quite done with the wax yet. Lifting from her appetizing tits, he sprinkled a trail of wax from the valley of her chest down to her navel. Rubbing against her center as every drop hit. Working in tandem, he passed her the candle and she blindly put it back on the table. Damond slid his body further down, while placing kisses and bites on the side of the trail he'd left, everything leading to the treat below. Placing his face against the sweetest part of her, he proceeded to love her with his tongue. Determined not to stop until she was outwardly as wild for him as he felt about her.

Janae had never gotten close to *thinking* about sex like this, not even in her dreams. All her nerve endings were screaming in bliss, and she gave a deep groan when his tongue hit her jewel, ran up and down her slit, probing in her secret place. Janae couldn't help scratching his shoulders, grabbing at his head, even as she tried to press her legs closed against his sensual assault. None of this to stop him mind you, but to press him even closer, she wanted to keep the pleasure going.

Shaking, bucking and crying out as she came *again*. Rocking against his tongue she clutched the pillow above her when her hand made contact with condom, and Janae wrapped her fingers around it urgently. Bringing it closer so she could see it with her blurred vision, she tore it open with shaky hands.

"Damond, I want you inside me *now*. I *need* you."

Seeing the condom he took it. "Don't worry, I plan to take care of all your needs tonight."

When he finally slid into her heat, she would swear her heart skipped a beat, when he moved it started thumping like a drum. Wrapping her legs high around his waist, Janae took each thrust he gave. Flowed with him as he rolled them over so she could ride him slow and steady, then hard and wild. Right before Damond pulled her down tight against his chest, kissing her breathless while pushing strongly up inside her.

When they broke—it was together. Skin to skin, mouth to mouth and heart to heart.

Chapter Eleven

The lights came back on while she was in the bathroom, having rushed inside as soon as Damond came out. She had thought about retreating while *he* was gone, but didn't trust herself not to fall down the steps in the dark. Not with the way her legs were still feeling like jelly. Now she was holding on to the sink looking at the woman in the mirror. A woman who looked as if she had been thoroughly ravaged.

And she had, just not in the way you would think. Janae had been expecting something more rough and tumble, instead she had gotten sensual and passionate. Something that had her stomach still quivering, her hands still shaky. Intellectually she knew most of it was the adrenaline still in her bloodstream, but the rest she gave sole credit to Damond. Stalling long enough, she gathered her robe tight and opened the door. And damn him for being propped up in bed looking right at her.

"I guess I should go back to my room..."

"You said you came here for both." Damond flipped the covers again. "Let me do my job and be your sleep buddy...for the night."

"But the lights-"

"Forget about the damn lights and get in this bed!"

Rolling her eyes, she walked forward only to have him shake his head.

"Without the polar bear robe, how the hell did you have room for that?"

Janae laughed and the light tension hovering in the room eased.

"I lined my suitcase with it and put everything else on top. I didn't know how cold it would be up here."

"Well, ditch it. I'll be keeping you warm."

Janae saw the intense flash of desire spark in his eyes before he banked it, and the following shiver that traveled her body had nothing to do with the temperature. For the second time she dropped the robe and hurried into bed, cuddling against his heated skin. He wrapped his arms around her and within a few seconds Janae felt relaxed. Soon her heartbeat evened out, and Janae actually felt like she could fall asleep even though it was barely ten p.m. The events of the night made everything feel so much later.

"Tell me something Professor, when was the last time you were with a man?"

Oh boy. "Why is that something you even want to know?"

"Humor me."

"It doesn't matter but almost two years." Janae was strangely embarrassed by her truth.

"It matters, no wonder you're so uptight."

Janae's head snapped up sharply. "You can't help yourself from saying offensive things can you?" She went to pull away, but he held on tight.

"I wasn't *trying* to be offensive just telling the truth. Nothing to get your feathers ruffled over." Damond smoothed a hand along her shoulder.

"Well, I don't appreciate it," Janae snapped. "How long has it been for *you*? I assume not long since you're traveling around with condoms."

"A smart woman like you should really stop making assumptions. I didn't come here *with* condoms. I bought them after an attractive but annoyingly serious professor broke into my house and refused to leave."

Janae didn't know which one she was more surprised at, the compliment or his admission about the condoms.

"I didn't break in. I had the code and you didn't answer the question."

"Keep telling yourself that. As for me...it's been nine months."

"Seriously? That's like two years in sexual terms for men. No wonder you-" She jerked her hand up and down. "You know, all the time."

"I do this." Damond repeated her hand motion while grinning. "Because it feels good, not because I'm hard up."

"Okay sure...whatever. Why has it been so long? You're good looking and charming when you want to be. Despite your habit of being blunt, I wouldn't think you'd have much trouble in the sex department."

The room was quiet while Damond decided if he was going to answer or not. She waited, her small hand playing with the little hairs on his chest.

"I broke up with my long-term girlfriend a year ago, and after a few months decided to get over her with a woman or two—warming my bed. And that was the last time I had some loving before I decided to go the celibate route and focus on my work...until tonight."

Janae was not anticipating that answer. The fact he'd been in a long-term relationship fairly recently, nor the faint hurt tinging his voice when he mentioned it. She doubted he realized he'd exposed a truth. That the women hadn't help ease the pain of his ex, and *that* was the real reason he'd decided to go without sex for so long.

Instead of saying any of that she asked instead, "How do you define long term?"

"We were together for a little over two years before we split." He clarified.

"Wow, I'm sorry."

"Don't be, it was time. What's *your* excuse for going without?"

"I don't know. I usually prefer to be dating or officially in a relationship before sex enters the picture. It all started to seem like more trouble than it was worth. Life happened and before I knew it almost two years had passed. The longer you go without...the easier it becomes not to think about it."

"Speak for yourself." Damond muttered

"Actually, why don't we stop speaking at all? I'm tired."

"Go to sleep then, no one's stopping you."

Damond could have been up writing now that the electricity was back, but had zero desire to be anywhere that wasn't up against her soft naked skin at the moment.

"I really should have a scarf for my head." Janae complained on a yawn after a few minutes of silence. "My hair is going to be so knotted tomorrow."

"Damnit, woman."

Grumbling, Damond got up pulling the head rag she'd left in the basement out the top dresser drawer. He tossed it to her before turning off the lights.

"I wondered where this disappeared to! You're a thief."

"I was going to give it back...eventually. Now put it on and let's go to bed."

"A rude thief at that." She noted, doing a sloppy braid of her hair, then slipping the silk on her head. The small ritual added some normalcy to their surreal situation.

"Thank you." She gave him a quick kiss on the mouth before snuggling against his side. Hoping he understood that the thanks was for more than a scarf.

* * *

The next morning Janae woke up alone, but with the smell of food wafting past her nose. Looking around the room for the rarity of a wall clock since she didn't have her cell, she actually found one and saw it was only nine in the morning. Gingerly rolling out of bed she donned her robe and crept down the steps, or so she thought. As soon as she hit the bottom Damond called out from the kitchen.

"Why don't you get settled and grab some of this food before it gets stone cold."

"Ummm...okay."

She ended up taking a quick shower when her body could have used a long hot soak, before joining him in the kitchen. He was done eating, but sat drinking a second cup of coffee, keeping her company while she ate. He barely looked like he was functioning which amused her since he was only up a few hours earlier than normal, not to mention he'd gone to bed *way* sooner than he usually did. Guess he really wasn't a morning person.

They had a slightly stilted conversation for twenty minutes before Damond announced he was about to catch up on writing. She agreed she would be doing the same and they parted ways. The rest of the day flowed mostly how the last one had, except they gravitated to the kitchen around dinner time instead of avoiding each other.

*

While they'd gone back to eating dinner nightly Damond didn't tease her, at least not sexually. They joked, debated and he was as vexing as ever. But what they *weren't* doing in the last five days was touching, kissing, or having sex between the sheets, or anywhere else for that matter.

At first, she was glad Damond hadn't thrown it in her face, an act she didn't put pass him. Though honestly she wasn't embarrassed at all. She had loved everything about their night together. *Literally* everything about it, from fooling around in the living room to what they'd done in the bedroom. It had all felt daring and exciting to her and frankly she wanted to do it again.

Janae considered herself a rational, realistic adult. While she hadn't foreseen them having sex, now that they had she saw no reason to put the cat back in the bag. Which ironically putting a feline in any container was hard as hell, almost as hard as pretending you hadn't had sex with a person you saw every day. Which told her Damond was going out of his way to act like it never happened.

This annoyed and even pissed her off a little. No woman wanted her sexuality to be ignored, plus she knew damn well he'd enjoyed it as much as she had. Yes, they both had work so she didn't expect them to go at it 24/7, like a couple of teenagers left alone for the weekend. But *five* days later and he hadn't leered at her, tried to grope her or given her even *one* suggestive comment. So tonight as they finished a perfectly enjoyable dinner and conversation, she confronted him. Blocking his path as he went to head out.

Damon looked at her distractedly. "Out of the way Professor, it's your night for the dishes."

"The dishes can wait."

That got his attention and he looked up from where he was writing notes in that little book.

"Something is more important to you than being clean and organized?"

"Stop it, I hate when you act like I have OCD. Having dirty dishes in the sink for a while won't hurt anything. I want to talk to you."

"Okay...no need to get touchy." He tucked his pen and notebook away and gave her his attention. "What is it? Though whatever it is the answer is most likely *no*."

Sometimes conversations with him felt like talking to an old grumpy man that wanted everyone off his lawn. Janae decided she'd be better off speaking his language—bluntness.

"Why haven't you tried to seduce me again?"

"Whoa, back up!" Damond actually took a step back giving her a once over. "I didn't seduce you the *first* time. Did you forget you offered me a hand-"

"Whatever, why haven't we slept together since last Saturday. You haven't even attempted..." Janae trailed off, feeling like a fool as he looked at her oddly. "Never mind."

"Wait." He pulled her back as she tried to leave. "How was I supposed to know you wanted to be together again? Hell, honestly Janae I figured you might want to forget it. I've been letting it ride, and frankly I should get an award for my good behavior."

Janae moved to stand very close to him. "I don't regret it and I don't want to forget it either."

"Draw me a map, cause I'm lost here." Damond ran a hand over his jaw in frustration. "What exactly do you want?"

"Only what you want to give." She told him truthfully.

"What I want to give? Well, I *have* been wanting to kiss you, but was afraid of getting a crook in my neck from kissing your short ass-"

"Forget it, you're never serious!"

"Damnit wait." Damond spun her around, lifting her up in the process and putting her on the kitchen island. "That's better."

Damond kissed her slowly, savoring the taste of her on his tongue. God this woman must be insane to think he hadn't thought about her day and night. Shit, he was eating dinner with her just to get an hour of her time each day, anything to be around her. Of course he'd noticed the looks she'd given him. How she managed to brush up against him at least *once* every time they shared space.

He'd been craving having her flesh in his hands and wanting to have her hips against his every day. Would have jumped her the morning after instead of cooking, if he had thought she was down for it. Janae had said she wasn't the fling type and that was all he had to give. Sucking on her bottom lip he eased back. Loving the dazed look he was able to put in her eyes.

"You were right before...I can't let this be a distraction."

Janae softly bit his lip. "Neither can I."

"My work..." He trailed his tongue down the soft column that was her neck. "It's important to my livelihood."

"So is mine." She moaned out as he squeezed a breast. "But weren't you the one who said sex gets the creative juices flowing."

Damond laughed low, and oh *so* damn sexy next to her ear. "That was me, wasn't it?"

"Yes, and now I concur with your assessment." Janae moved her hand in between them, grabbing his hard shaft. "I can see it already has *something* flowing in you."

"Damn right!" Damond took her mouth again, lifting her up until she wrapped those sexy legs around him. "Enough talk."

"I couldn't agree more." Janae clung to his neck. "I want more action."

Chapter Twelve

Damon was bordering on exhaustion. Little Ms. Buttoned Up was wearing his ass out. He wasn't actually complaining, what man would? He was just stating a fact. For close to two weeks now they were running around having sex everywhere in between working. Her room, his, the room she had taken as her office, the basement couch—everywhere. He'd even had a first for him, finishing what they'd started on that pool table, and let's just say he'd never look at the game the same way again.

The odd thing was their sexual frenzy *did* seem to increase work production. Words and storylines where coming to him easier than ever before, while she had sorted and laid out eighty percent of her book already. Hell, if he had known having regular hot sex with a college educator who wore her hair in a severe bun was all it took, he would have hired a woman for role-play months ago. Damond wanted to fool himself but knew most likely not just *anyone* would have worked.

It was something about Janae that stimulated his mental and sexual nerves. He enjoyed their debates and poking at her. He also enjoyed the down time where they just hung out and relaxed. Recently they'd even started talking more in-depth about their work, something he had never done with Veronica. He'd tried a time or two but she responded by being visibly bored. His ex hadn't been a big reader of *anything* much less his genre, and didn't want to hear it.

It was cool to talk to another writer, one who read fiction here and there among other things instead of getting all their content off Twitter and Instagram. How he ended up with such a basic woman, *and* lasted so long with her was baffling? To be fair, Veronica was good looking and fun. A full five years his junior, she had been impressed with his casual lifestyle when they first met. His freedom of time as well as his money to live comfortably with an unconventional job had been right up her alley.

But Veronica had expensive taste that grew while they were together. And the constant fun from their first six months started to annoy him, plus the fact that she didn't have more drive and direction in life. Somehow, she'd still convinced him to allow her to move in, and things slowly but steadily started going downhill.

Veronica did temporary administrative work for a living. Assignments that lasted anywhere from three to six months, occasionally longer. She had told him she preferred it that way, that she turned down temp to hire positions. Spouted that foolishness about not wanting to be tied down to a corporation that only used her for what she could do for them. In the two years they dated she'd had six different jobs.

Damond could rock with her on not wanting to work for Uncle Sam, but the rest was bullshit. He was all for someone making their own path in life and doing what they loved. If she had pursued her own craft or business he would have backed and supported that completely. Instead, to him it looked like she wanted a ride through life. Frankly he must have been out of his mind to stay with her for so long.

Okay hell who was he kidding, she had left him. Veronica found a better sugar daddy to provide her with an even better lifestyle than he could. Probably a guy who didn't push her about wanting more out of life then *chilling*. But all that noise was in his past where it rightfully belonged. *Now* he was dealing with a person who didn't understand the meaning of a closed door.

"I'm working here, what do you want?" He asked, as Janae barged into the office.

"Just bringing you some tea. I just got done with my lunch and thought you could use some."

"You're trying to give me a bladder infection with all this tea. It has me running to the bathroom every other second."

"Stop exaggerating, I barely get you to drink a cup a day. I made you the wild sweet orange kind that you like so stop complaining. Also, you don't get a bladder infection from peeing, but from holding it in. Tea helps flush out toxins-"

Damond quickly lifted the cup and took a sip, glaring. "Happy now? Shut the door on the way out, I was just getting into a scene."

"You can be *sooo* grumpy sometimes. Anyway, have a good afternoon." Smiling widely Janae walked out.

He took another sip almost against his will, and admitted he really did like this flavor. It was just as well she had interrupted him from thinking about her and past relationships. Not that what they had was a relationship...it was more like a situationship at best.

"Fuck me."

Putting the tea aside, Damond was determined to push *all* women out of his head for the next few hours. He had a goal to finish his book before the week was out then start on its sequel.

*

Janae jogged upstairs humming, she enjoyed breeching his man cave of an office just to annoy him. At the same time trying to convince herself she wasn't mothering him, which he accused her of doing more than once. True, she did bother him about eating three complete meals a day and to drink less coffee, but it wasn't like she was picking out his underwear for him.

Women were natural nurturers, she was just helping another human in her living space.

Regardless, she didn't feel like his mother when they were in bed together, or on the floor or in the shower for that matter. God, what Damond was doing to her body was amazing! One guy in her first relationship out of college had called her a cold fish because she wouldn't suck his dick their first time having sex, claiming she needed to loosen up. Janae hated to admit it, but that assholes comment influenced her to a small extent, in every other relationship she had. Which was part of the reason she was normally slow to move into the sexual arena.

Once she did go there, things were usually fine. Not amazing like what she had with Damond, but adequate none the less. She had thought having decent to good sex was "normal". Many medical and pop culture articles showed that the majority of women were overall experiencing the same— just okay experiences. Sure, she knew that some folks were out there having amazing sex, but they weren't as plentiful as the TV shows and movies would have you believe. It was no coincidence that the rates of cheating were through the roof as folks searched for that elusive *bomb ass sex*. Somehow, she had found her person in a remote cabin up north.

She felt like an archeologist finding a temple of hidden treasure, and she was determined to get as much as possible while she could. Aside from sex there were other perks that Damond gave her. As she'd discovered from the start he was a great, if confrontational conversationalist. She loved that they could talk about a wide variety of topics, from something light to ultra-serious but never boring. Not to mention it was almost a guarantee that he would say something outlandish. Either amusing, annoying or sparking her mind to think deeper, Janae honestly loved it. Most men didn't realize it, but women could get turned on a *lot* by mental stimulation alone.

She tried to remind herself that this was all temporary. Janae had two more weeks to go before going home, which she tried not to think about. Wanting to enjoy this closeness, this experience she was having without ruining it with thoughts of the future. For once she was going to fully immerse herself in the unexpected. Her current make-believe reality.

The reality where she relished how they slept together each night, though they never started out that way. Sometimes he would come to her, and sometimes she would be the one to give in first, an odd little game of wills they played. Weird, but that was their entire relationship. Sometimes they fell right to sleep, making love in the morning instead. Then there were times they barely said a word before jumping each other. Other times they only talked into the night while snuggled up.

Janae would never pretend those moments didn't make her feel close to him. Just as close as their daily little domestic situations did. Like the tea today or how they ended up sharing a cart the last time they went to the store. Rolling down each aisle like a couple, her with a list and him randomly grabbing things, much like she imagined a married couple might.

"Get a grip girl. Damond is not the marrying kind."

Then again, she wasn't so sure. Out of the two of them he was the one who'd had the longest relationship. For her it had been a year and a half, though the guy had suddenly had a problem with her after she got her doctorate. For whatever reason that had rubbed him the wrong way, even though it was necessary for her chosen career path. It wasn't like she was one of those people trying to collect degrees just for the hell of it. She had been devastated for a brief time, somehow missing how insecure he was before that moment. Shella had barely resisted saying *I told you so*, even though she had. Her cousin had met him three times and never liked him from the start.

Apparently, Damond had been in another long-term relationship before this last one. Going *three and a half years* with that woman. He chalked it up to early adulthood as he'd been twenty-five at the time, but to her mind that wasn't *that* young. Janae was of the belief he enjoyed having a partner in his life. That instead of the lone wolf she had originally taken him for, he was a pack animal after all. She was the one who couldn't seem to connect long term to any man, and *that* thought was outright depressing.

Chapter Thirteen

When Janae came back downstairs around four that day, she ducked her head inside his office only to find he wasn't there. Frowning, she called out but didn't get a response. She even peaked her head in the basement but he wasn't there either. Going back upstairs she found it a little odd that he wasn't working this time of day, and he hadn't come upstairs for a nap. That third step from the top would have given him away, or he would have tried enticing her into some afternoon delight. No, she didn't think he was in the house at all.

Going into the kitchen, she got herself a bottle of water and wondered if maybe he had left. Taking a quick peek out the front window showed it was a calm, sunny winter's day. The last snow had been over four days ago, and was almost completely melted now. True, it was later in the day than he normally would have driven somewhere. But the days were already shifting, the light lingering longer than when she'd first arrived at the cabin. Which meant he could reasonably go somewhere and be back before dark.

Her contention was that he could have told her before leaving? No sooner than the thought hit her conscious, she cut it off. He was a grown able-bodied man, who despite the fact they were sleeping together was not *her* man. He could come and go as he pleased. Still, she was annoyed. Leaving the water, Janae went to put on her coat and boots. Heading down to the basement, she used the connecting door to enter the garage. Telling herself she would just take a quick peek and see if his car was still here. It was, and her budding anger moved into concern.

"Where the heck is he?"

Clicking the door opener, she waited as it rose and immediately saw him about 150 feet away, standing with his back to her. She walked out wondering why he hadn't turned at the sound of the door, he wasn't *that* far away. Instead he just stood there, kind of swaying. Starting out towards him, something made Janae go to the side of the garage instead.

She rarely came outside unless they were leaving the house, she just wasn't a fan of the cold and snow. It was a wonder she had survived her entire life in Michigan. The state's saving grace were the terrific summers which made up for winter. But Janae figured since she was out here, it was a good time to look at the generator. She hadn't forgotten about it, just currently distracted with work and sex. It was right where Damond said it would be, and one quick glance showed that it wasn't plugged in properly. Bending down she quickly took care of the issue.

Janae watched as the indicator lights on top flashed on. The thing looked in fine working order to her, had he unplugged this? Though she knew it was "possible" it had been knocked out some other way, it was highly unlikely. These things were built exactly so random disconnecting wouldn't happen. Spinning on her heels she started marching towards him through the slushy snow. He still hadn't turned around, and just that quickly Janae went from suspicious anger to concern again. Was he ill? When she was ten feet away still nothing, just the light swaying she had noticed from the house.

"Damond?" She lightly touched his shoulder. "Are you okay?"

"What the-"

When he swung around wildly, she had to quickly step back to avoid his reach.

"It's just me! What is wrong with you?"

Damond vaguely heard her words, he definitely saw her mouth moving as he yanked out his earbuds.

"Jesus woman, don't you know not to sneak up on a man like that?"

"I didn't know I was. I had no clue you were listening to music, I didn't see them."

"They're cordless." He held up one giving her a "duh" look.

"How was I supposed to know that? You're the one standing out here like a mental patient swaying. I thought you'd had some type of medical emergency. Especially after you never turned around when I opened the garage door *or* walked over."

"Fine, my bad. Just next time yell or something. I didn't know who was touching me. You could have gotten knocked out."

Now Janae smirked. "Why so jumpy? Aren't you the one always telling me there's no murderers out here."

"Yeah, well one can never be too careful, can they?"

"Hmm, what *are* you doing out here? I got worried when I couldn't find you in the house."

"Missing me huh?"

"No, just concerned and you haven't answered my question yet."

He still didn't, bending down instead to pick up the pen and notepad he'd dropped, before waving it in her face.

"I came out to clear my head." He left out that thoughts of her kept interrupting him all afternoon. "It was working. Zoning out on music and putting some plot points down. Until *you*, nosey goldilocks came out here trying to give me a heart attack."

"Well, if you had left a note...I wouldn't have come looking for you. I'm just glad you're okay. It's cold. *I'm* going back inside."

When she turned to leave, he pulled her into his chest, crossing his arms behind her back.

"It's cute you care about my safety."

"No, it was self-preservation. If a psycho had taken you out, I was probably next."

"You're a liar, Professor." Damond gave her a peck on the lips which she returned. "And not a good one."

"Takes one to know one Mr. Hall. Speaking of which, I finally got a chance to take a look at the generator."

"Really..." Damond turned his head to the side.

Janae promptly moved it back with a finger. "Yes, really. You want to know what I found?"

"Not, but it seems like you want to tell me."

"The cord wasn't connected to the other thing that goes into the house."

"Imagine that?"

She pushed, not so gently away from his hold. "I'm betting you don't have to imagine it. You saw it the night the lights went out."

"I barely saw shit that night, between the dark and the foot of snow."

"Admit it." Janae crossed her arms. "You unplugged the generator didn't you? Be honest."

"No, I didn't unplug it." He shook his head, looked at her and then on a sigh continued. "But I didn't hook it up either. When I got out there, I saw it was unplugged and left it that way."

"I can't believe you did that!" She sprung forward hitting his chest a couple of times. "You knew how afraid I was. Why would you do that?"

Damond caught her flying hands and held them with one of his own, pulling her closer until he could wrap his arms around her again.

"I did it because I wanted to spend time with you, wanted you in my arms."

Janae was speechless. "You couldn't have just told me that, *after* the lights were running?"

"Would you have listened? We were avoiding each other, but I couldn't stop thinking about you. So I figured you being scared would drive you into my arms...and it did."

"To think you've accused *me* of being juvenile."

"Touché Professor. But a man suffering from blue balls doesn't think so clearly."

Janae kicked his shin. "You should be ashamed of yourself."

"You know that hurt, right." Tightening his hold, Damond pressed a lingering kiss to her pouting mouth. Not pulling back until he felt them soften.

"You should investigate that violent streak you have, write about yourself in your book." Damond tried teasing.

"You are incorrigible. I don't know whether to feel duped or plain angry."

Damond's shrewd eyes grew serious, something they rarely were. His cold gloved hand, caressed the side of her face. Startling her even more then his look.

"We both know you didn't come to my bed just because the lights were out, don't cheapen what we shared that night. And I'm not ashamed, I'd do it all over again. Hell, I'd take a hammer to the damn thing if it meant us having the last few weeks together. Would you want to miss out on that?"

"You know I don't. I went to your room because I wanted to. Because I wanted to be *with* you. But Damond...don't ever outright lie to me again. Got it?"

"I hear you and I won't." Kissing her forehead he asked, "Will you dance with me Janae."

"What?" Even now he could make her laugh, sometimes he was so ridiculous.

Damond focused on programing his phone for a moment, then placed one earbud firmly in her ear, the other in his. Janae heard Babyface's "Sorry for the Stupid Things" flow into her eardrum and laughed even harder, giving him a real smile. Stepping into his waiting arms, hers going around his waist as they stood two-stepping in the snow. In a world that held only the two of them.

Chapter Fourteen

They danced until the song ended, which flowed into a kiss before one of their feet slipped and they almost fell.

"Let's head in," Damond suggested. "Your lips are turning blue. I can't have you catching frostbite."

"Same for you." She squeezed in-between his legs. "Or at least the parts of you I'm not finished using."

"You got a lot of nerve lady." But Damond was talking to himself as Janae took off.

He followed more slowly, until he saw her letting the garage door down and he tried to speed up. Not that he made it, so he had to walk all the way around to the front door. By the time he was inside and undressed he found her already in the living room. Sipping on a hot beverage of undetermined flavor.

"Did you make me some?"

"No."

"Ain't that a bit-" He cut off as she gave him a look. "I'm just saying...I was out there longer than you were."

"That sounds like a personal problem." Janae surmised.

"And I think you're a little vindictive."

Damond dropped down next to her and promptly took her cup. Gulping down a good portion of what turned out to be peppermint tea before she snatched it back.

"And you, Mr. Wannabe James Patterson, are a bit of an asshole."

"Is that the clinical term for it, Professor?"

"No, your type of assholery falls into the Machiavellianism diagnoses."

"Hmmm, I like it. I'd like permission to use that line in a book." Damon asked even as he was already scribbling it down.

"Go right ahead. I plan to cite your name when I talk about anti-social behavior." Janae retorted dryly.

"Remember how I was thinking about having a female psychologist in my new series. I want you to be the consultant for me. I mean I've looked up some things, made up some. But I have you right here. Do you have an hour to go over some key scenes that I've written? Assess the lingo, and the thought process my doc might have."

"You really want to pick my brain?" Janae eyebrows lifted in surprise.

"On the head shrink part, yes."

"Okay, fine. I can give you until dinner to help you out, but you have to cook *and* do the dishes."

"Like I said...vindictive." He proclaimed shaking his head.

* * *

It was a week later and Janae was up in her office mad at the world. It was an unreasonable thought, she recognized that and still she hated everybody. After the first couple of slow weeks her work had taken off, which made sense. She had only needed to stitch her work and concepts together into a readable, interesting and teachable book.

Now with about ten percent left, she only needed to summarize everything, but was suddenly thrown for a loop. Janae had covered a lot of ground on her topic and didn't know where to start. But she hadn't written more than two paragraphs in the five hours she had been up here today. Using the time instead to pour over other chapters. Double and triple checking some of her research facts. Making slight changes to some sections even though this wasn't the time for editing.

"Dang it! Why is my brain fritzing out now?"

Slamming back from the table she got to her feet and started a stomping version of pacing.

"I want this to be done, but I'm worried about the peer review," Janae said to the air.

When someone a few years back with similar perspectives as hers published, a few people had tried to poke holes in every theory.

"Jesus, I so hate the damn peer review system."

Janae flung a pillow from the bed to the other side of the room, as if that would hurt anything or even make her feel better.

*

Damond turned his eyes to the ceiling again. This was twice now he'd heard her tramping around up there. He was starting to wonder what the hell was going on, she normally wasn't this noisy. What had started as an irritation now had him curious. This time he finally stood up.

"Let's go see what the Professor is up to."

If she had been in her bedroom downstairs he might have thought she was packing. He was intently aware she only had one more week with him, or rather at the cabin. Damond could see Janae being an early packer, one of those people who re-checked a hotel room before they left. He was trying not to think on it too much—her leaving that is. Odd, when she'd first arrived *all* he could think about was how slow eight weeks would go by. Taking the steps two at a time he reached her door and gave a quick knock.

"Hey, you cool in there?"

"Please go away. I'm busy. I don't have time to...play."

Damond would have left if her voice hadn't sounded so tight and upset. He took a risk and decided to open the door any way.

"Sounds like you could use a quick bre-"

He faltered taking a quick look around the room. Seeing pillows strewn about, numerous papers and open books everywhere. Even when writing she was neat, and he'd never seen her work area no matter where it was look like this.

"What in the world are you doing in here?" He was truly puzzled and became more so when she burst out in tears at his question.

"I don't know what I'm doing, that's the problem!" Wiping her eyes as she walked to the window.

Damond was stunned. What in the holy hell was going on? Shit he hated a crying woman, it seemed like he never had a clue what was actually wrong.

"Janae, tell me what happened…"

Tears still streaming she snapped around.

"Everything is wrong! I'm almost done with this book. I've worked hard and you know what…it won't be good enough. Someone will go out of their way to disprove it or parts of it. What makes it even worse is the fact I'll *still* have to write another, and another. All to prove I know my shit, even after all that damn education I'm still paying for. Just to stay relevant in my field *and* have any hope of being tenured."

Janae threw her hands up and started sobbing in earnest. "I'm tired of keeping up. So damn tired, and yet there's never any rest!"

"Baby come here." Giving her a hug, he wiped her cheeks. "What's with the tears? You don't cry at strange, naked assholes in your cabin, my constant teasing or my snide remarks. Don't let this break you."

"It's my work! I'm so close to being finished and tying it all together, but now I've hit a mental roadblock. Then that got me thinking was any of it good?" Janae left his arms and started pacing again.

"This time around it's *only* my name on it. No one or anything to hide behind. When folks in my specialty start picking it apart, it will be *my* concepts and ideas and knowledge they're dissecting."

Damond sat on the bed and listened, when she took a big enough pause he finally jumped in.

"Let me ask you a few simple questions. One, do you consider what you've written to be accurate to the best of your knowledge and research?"

"Yes, of course I do! I wouldn't go around pulling facts from the air."

"Two, do you believe your book flows and makes logical sense in the order that you've mapped it out?"

"Yes." Now she frowned, finally coming to a standstill. "I've made sure that each chapter flows into the next as an easy transition, and builds on what was discussed in the previous chapters."

"Great, now last question. And this one is easy. Do you believe you've done your best?"

"Absolutely. I would never *not* do my best on anything, much less a text teaching and giving information to others."

"Well, there you have it." Damond tossed up his hands. "Come here." He waved her over until he could pull her down next to him.

"Don't let self-doubt win, that bastard plagues writers, often when we're near the finish line. It's as if the weeks, months and for some years, spent working on their manuscript is suddenly all trash. It's not. You have high standards, you would never put out anything subpar."

"I wouldn't, would I. Thanks for saying that." Janae burrowed into his side, feeling calmer already.

"What you need is a new perspective." Damond rubbed her back. "Focus on what you *have* accomplished already, not what you haven't. Give yourself a break and then make a plan for wrapping this project up. Cut it into smaller sections if need be."

"Smaller tasks to complete a whole, *are* less stressful. I needed that reminder. Ugh, I think this is just my post period hormones and stress." Janae wiped under her still dripping nose. "It's only been finished for a day and a half, so my hormones are still fluctuating."

Damon was thankful her birth control made the time as short as it was, not to mention happy to know it was done with. It had been the longest five days.

"Thanks for the gynecology lesson."

"You're welcome." She poked his shoulder. "Thank *you* for listening."

"No problem. Make sure I don't need to do it again. I suck at being Mr. Sensitive."

"Aww, I think you did great." Janae praised him. "I'm impressed."

"Yeah, well don't get used to it. We should get back to work."

Chapter Fifteen

After her talk with Damond Janae felt much better and chopped the last chapter down into sections to tackle one at a time. It was nice to have someone who understood writing and how it could twist you up inside or bounce her concerns off of. The fact that he hadn't dismissed her feelings as being dramatic was unexpected. He'd been able to comfort her and give her a kick in the pants at the same time. Janae was able to settle into work so well, that she lost track of time, and didn't hear him until he was knocking on her door once again.

"Come in."

"I was waiting for you to come to dinner but you never did."

A quick glance at her phone showed it was already 6:45.

"Sorry, I completely lost track of time." Janae apologized. "I hope you didn't start cooking. I'll whip up something for tonight."

"Don't worry about it. That's not why I came up. I'm putting on some clothes so we can go out. I'd tell you to do the same but you look fine."

"Out? Where to?"

"I'm taking you to dinner. And don't ask too many questions before I change my mind. Give me about thirty minutes and I'll meet you downstairs."

"Okay...." But she was already speaking to his back as he left.

Looking down at her clothes, Janae rushed down the steps to her bedroom. He was taking her out on a date and she couldn't stop smiling. Damond was often gruff and at times could be even cynical, but she'd learned over the last few weeks that he could be downright sweet as well. Jumping out of a quick shower, she took her hair down. Smoothing the waves and curls with some leave-in conditioner before turning her attention on what to wear.

She wanted to look pretty for him tonight, to do something special, just as he was going out of his way to cheer her up. She hadn't foreseen having a hot affair with a man while she was up here and had only brought basic underwear with her. Not that he had complained as he preferred her completely naked. But Janae wanted to look more feminine for him, sexy.

Not long after they'd started sleeping together, she had bugged him until he'd taken her to the closest mall. True she could have driven herself, but she had grown accustomed to being chauffeured. As a modern woman Janae told herself she should be ashamed, but it could be tiring doing everything on your own, 24/7. Having someone to do half the meals, drive and an ear to talk to, felt wonderful. Just knowing there was another "option" besides *do it yourself* took a lot of pressure off.

After he'd grumbled for show they'd headed out to Station Mall which wasn't that far from the center of town, but did happen to be on the other side of the St. Mary's River—on the Canadian side. It had felt good to get out the cabin and also have a little slice of *city*. They'd agreed to meet back up in forty-five minutes and parted ways. She hadn't wanted him to see what she was buying because where was the surprise in that. Hitting the first women's clothing store she ran across, Janae wasn't impressed. Luckily the next place had a better selection. A red and black satin and lace underwear set, plus a slinky long sleeve dress shirt had caught her eye.

Tonight, she would get to wear both purchases. While getting dressed she remembered the rest of that day. Once they'd met back up he'd surprised her by asking if she wanted to catch a movie at the mall theatre. She'd easily agreed not even minding the action packed one he picked. Even laughing when he convinced her to sneak some food from New York Fries inside her purse for them to eat. They'd had fun, eventually checking out a few more stores together before leaving for home. If she really thought about it, that *could* count as their first date. Either way, she was excited that he had initiated dinner out.

* * *

Damond didn't know what the hell he'd been thinking organizing this outing. But leaving her earlier today he'd been disturbed by the encounter. Crying didn't suit the Professor at all, and he hadn't liked it. Seeing that vulnerable raw side to her made him both uncomfortable and cranky for no reason, and all he could think about was putting a smile on her face. He'd take that lofty bored expression she sometimes used to ignore his antics, over a sad and defeated look in her eyes any day. Which was why he'd hopped on the internet and started looking for places to eat until he found something she might like. Damond was now downstairs waiting for her to come out, and the wait was well worth it.

She had on a pair of jeans that he was sure he'd never seen before, because who could forget something that molded hips and ass to perfection. The red shimmery top, hung off one shoulder making him instantly think of licking the exposed skin. But it was her hair that stole the show, left loose and pinned up on one side, only to cascade down the other. It made her look young and sexy. He was sure she could rival the students she taught.

"You look great."

"Thank you. I hope I didn't keep you waiting."

"It wouldn't matter." Damond ran his eyes slowly over her so she could see the appreciation in them. "It was worth it. Let me help with your coat."

Janae was touched *and* surprised how his simple solicitous behavior had butterflies flitting around in her stomach. Like she'd told him after their first time together, he could be charming when he wanted to. In the car Damond kept the conversation light, keeping her laughing with jokes and crazy stories. They both steered away from work and just enjoyed the serene drive into town.

"Where are we eating?" Janae finally asked. "I'm just now realizing that I'm *very* hungry."

"You'll see when we get there, which should be any minute now. I think you'll like it."

"As long as they have food, I'll be good."

Janae rethought that comment as they pulled into what seemed like a plaza parking lot. The outside of Fuji Japanese Steak House & Sushi was not impressive, but she plastered a smile on her face as he came to let her out. She did like sushi, and she was famished, so taste was her main concern right now. Luckily inside was *much* better. The bright colors at the bar area, contrasted with the rest of the dimly lit restaurant giving it a nice ambiance.

As she looked around spying on what people had on their plates, Damond had a brief conversation with a server, before they were led to a two-person table in a corner. It was the most privacy they would get in this casual dining setting and it was perfect in her mind. Settling down with menus, Damond quickly ordered some miso soup and a spicy salmon roll as starters. Only turning to her once the waiter was gone.

"Damn, sorry I didn't mean to order for you, I should have asked."

"It's okay this time. I happen to love both those things." Seeing his shoulders relax, Janae reached across the table to briefly squeeze his hand.

"Plus, I'm starving. Thanks for making sure food will get in my stomach sooner than later."

"You're welcome...I'm definitely ready to eat myself."

Janae's face heated because he wasn't looking at the menu but at her. She had been keenly aware of missing his loving once her period started, at the same time appreciating him not making a fuss about it. Damond had come to her room every night to rub her back. Though she'd felt fine, the hardheaded man had insisted. After feeling slightly put out, she'd felt taken care of, just like she did today. When their drinks arrived and they put in their main meals—the Hibachi steak and shrimp for him and the chicken and salmon for her—she turned to thank him again.

"This was a nice surprise Damond. But you didn't have to go out of your way because I had a meltdown."

"Don't flatter yourself Professor, I wanted some steak. Plus, I didn't want to chance you throwing something and putting a hole in my wall. Remember, I'm invested in the upkeep of that place."

"Whatever you say." She let him play it off. "By the way, thanks to your counsel I got a decent amount done after you left, so I'm feeling good about my progress and finishing before I leave."

"Yeah? Well good, that's only six days away."

Janae laughed. "Don't tell me you're counting the days until I'm out your hair."

"Not quite." His tone was somber, before he changed the subject. "What's next for you once you get back?"

"Well..." She cleared her throat from the brief, but heavy moment. "I'll have a couple of months to review and edit, then send it off to a professional set of eyes. I'll be teaching one spring and summer class to make up for lost time. Classes start in May. Once my book is as good as it's going to get, I send it off for the peer review, *they* have up to six weeks to look at it. Then my hope is to make it available for my fall classes."

Damond's eyebrows rose. "In other words, no rest for the weary."

"Exactly." Janae played with her chopsticks, the reminder that their time was ending making her appetite wane. "How about you, aren't you almost done?"

"Yeah I am, should be done before this week is out with book one. Then I'll immediately start work on the next. I'd like to have both done if possible before I hit the road. Then much like you, I'll start the revision process. I'm hoping to have the first one published however by early August. Then release the second by December."

"You will. Don't hope, just claim it."

Damond smirked. "Now you sound like my grandmother. She used to always say that."

"Didn't *all* our grandmothers say that? But I have found that mind over matter can actually work and there is science behind visualization techniques. You know seeing yourself in a situation and succeeding ahead of time. Did you know they often teach this to athletes, as a way to psych them up and win?"

"No, I didn't. Tell me more, actually don't. It might ruin sports for me."

"How would it?" Chuckling she rolled her eyes at him. "Help me understand your logic."

That steered them into one of their friendly debates, and away from talk about serious things like work and leaving their secluded cabin. When the main dishes came she asked to taste his shrimp and steak. And after chastising her on ordering the healthy option but wanting to eat *real food*, they ended up swapping half their meal with the other. Damond scowling the entire time, while she hummed happily eating slices of his beef. It was an enjoyable night and she was actually sad to leave their small romantic corner when they left.

Taking control of the radio she found some old school R&B and let it play as they rode home, mostly in silence. She had no clue what he was thinking, but her mind was wishing it didn't have to end so soon. Looking up at the open sky helped quiet her unhappy thoughts. Here, there were no buildings or lights, to block or outshine the stars, and it was beautiful. Peaceful, simple and relaxing.

Janae still couldn't see herself ever living out here permanently, but she had a renewed appreciation for nature and the serenity of it all. She knew life worked in cycles. That anything with a start had an end, but she was determined to enjoy *every bit* of it while she could.

Chapter Sixteen

As they came down the lane to the large cabin, she was struck again by how quickly things change. The first time coming down this stretch of road Janae thought she might have lost her mind. And now look, it had turned into her own little love shack. Janae hadn't been looking for it, but it had been what she needed. All Janae wanted now was to get inside and warm up by getting close and personal with one Damond Hall.

Once inside Damond hung up their coats, while shuffling his feet like a school boy on his first date. In fact he felt exactly like that, and it made him feel ridiculous. He didn't know if he should make the first move or wait for her. Thankfully, she turned around and slid into his arms, raising up on her toes to give him a gentle kiss.

"Thanks again for everything. I really enjoyed dinner and appreciate everything you did for me today."

"It's not a big deal."

"Uh-uh." Placing a finger against his lips she stopped his self-deprecation. "Just say, you're welcome."

"You're welcome." He obediently repeated. "How do you want to spend the rest of the night?"

"Why don't you go make us a fire, we can sit on that horrid rug. I'll go freshen up and be back in a little bit."

"Sounds like a plan."

He watched her switch away and knew someone was feeling frisky. Fine by him, he was certainly up for playing with her kitty-cat. Hell, he was hoping to *stroke* it all night long. With that idea in mind he ran up to his own room to hit the can, before grabbing a few condoms. He didn't want any interruptions once they got going, they had time to make up. Coming down Damond got the fire going in time to hear her door open. Peeking down the hall, he waved her forward as she veered for the kitchen.

"I was going to grab some wine." Janae explained.

"I'll take care of it. You just relax and get comfortable."

"Well, you don't have to tell me twice." Looked like her night of pampering would continue.

Fully coming into the living room as he was leaving, she noticed the condoms on the table and the couple of pillows he'd placed on the floor so they could sit. Making a split decision as a giggle bubbled up, Janae went for it. When Damond did come back with a glass of red wine in each hand, he almost spilled them at what he saw.

"*Damnnnn*. Doesn't look like I needed to bother with the drinks, you already loose..."

"You said get comfortable, I took you to heart."

Janae was laying on the couch propped up on her side, in just the new bra and panties. Damond didn't say anything else, just set both wine glasses on the table and slowly backed away. His eyes traveling over her body.

"You stay right there. *I'm* going to need something stronger than wine."

Janae felt keyed up as Damond went to the side cart stocked with premium liquor. He took a decanter of bourbon and poured a glass before walking into the kitchen for ice. Pausing on his way to stare at her again, all while shaking his head slowly in disbelief.

Janae used the time to drink half of her own wine, then went back to what she hoped was a casual yet sexy pose. She tried not to overthink why he hadn't pounced on her yet and decided to let everything play out. Damond's mind worked in mysterious ways. When he came back, he was slowly sipping as he strutted proudly out the kitchen completely naked.

"I felt overdressed for this party." He explained at seeing her expression.

Yet he still didn't come join her, lowering himself to the rug in front of the fire instead.

"Should I join you?" Janae offered.

"No baby, you're perfect where you are. I'm trying to look my fill because when I touch you all that tantalizing material is coming off in a hurry."

"So you like it?"

"Are you insane, of course I like it! Get up and show off for me."

Janae finished off her glass, needing it as she stood up to model for him. Her thought process was; she would wear it, he would see it, *then* they would devour each other. Another reminder how different men and women thought, and this man in particular always seemed to confound her.

Standing slowly, she took a few steps until she cleared the table so he could see all of her, then decided to have fun with it. Twirling around and putting hands to hips as she posed. Stretching her arms overhead so that her stomach was taunt, both breasts lifting up and out. Then slowly trailed one hand down the other arm, moving her hips sensually side to side. After a moment or two she really got into it, even turning around, shaking her ass at him a little. The entire time his eyes were on her like a hot brand. Janae would swear she actually felt heat as his eyes roamed over her skin, and it made her feel more lightheaded than the wine.

Damond considered they may have been abducted by aliens on that dark ride home. It was a good explanation for what was happening now. They were probably in holding pods, while the aliens put them in a combined dream state. He couldn't figure out another way to explain her being dressed to bring a man to his knees. Or how he was lucky enough to get this *sexy as fuck* show. He knew the moment she really let go, having to grip the rug beneath him so he didn't do the same to his cock. Taking another big swallow from his glass he finally set it down before shifting.

"Thanks. You've just given me quite an education on "how to drive a man wild without even touching him". I'm impressed with your teaching style."

"Good, there might be a test later, so you should study hard."

"I have a feeling I'm going to pass." Damond smirked. "I have an inappropriate relationship with the teacher. Now take that off and come over here."

She pouted a little. "You're not going to do it for me?"

"Since this is the first time I'm seeing that set I have a feeling you bought it recently. I'd hate to rip it to shreds in my impatience to get to *every* inch of your skin."

When he lifted his shuttered eyelids, the raw desire she saw there almost made her take a step back. It unquestionably had her nerves tingling with all kinds of awareness. Before her was a predator of a man and it both thrilled her and made her feel in danger. Swallowing she unhooked the back of the bra, and as she pushed her panties down both pieces fell off her body.

Kneeling in front of him, their eyes locked as he leaned forward for a kiss. Janae's heart just about leapt from her chest, even though he pressed softly at first, the knowledge of what was to come still shot through her body. Damond was palming her nape, pulling her in, moving the kiss by degrees into something deeper.

Jesus, he hadn't felt this close to blowing his stack prematurely since he was fifteen. He'd seen many women in sexy lingerie and appreciated them all, but it was something about seeing Janae so sexually carefree and playful, that turned him on a hundred times more. Part of him wanted to languish in this moment, while the beast inside him wanted to take everything she offered—immediately and repeatedly. Pulling back he sat up, brushing the hair from her face.

"You've been hot to trot since we got back. I think you need to be cooled down."

"Is that really what you think Damond?" Janae caressed his thigh.

"Yeah it is, now close your eyes."

She let her eyes fall shut before sensing him move. Heard clinking before he shifted again, sliding his skin against hers as he laid next to her. Janae eagerly waited in anticipation of whatever came next.

Damond slid the ice cube from the bourbon on the underside of her breast first and watched her eyes pop open as she squealed.

"Keep those eyes closed, you're horrible at following directions."

An incredulous giggle rose out of her, as she did what she was told. "That's because *you're* crazy."

"You still sound too heated. We'll have to do something about that."

Damond ran the quickly melting ice over her warm brown areola, bringing her nipple to a point. Putting what was left of the icicle in his mouth, he drew her in next. Stopping the laughter in its tracks as she moaned. Damond suckled her as if he hadn't eaten a full meal less than an hour before, only to start again with a new ice cube on her other breast.

He had one more piece of ice left and he used that to run it down her stomach, circling her navel before lightly slipping it between her curls. He didn't stop as she cried out, continuing to graze her already firm bud of nerves. The ice melted, running down into her plump folds, making her shake and groan.

He reached for a condom next, struggling to put it on as she was all over him, licking his neck and grabbing his ass. Somehow, he got the task done, all while giving her a kiss that neither would soon forget.

That was when his beast won the war to be inside her.

Directing Janae to all fours he penetrated her wet sheath—the flames from the fire assaulting his back as he pounded into her. All while her hips eagerly met his, and still it wasn't enough. It never seemed to be when it came to her, and tonight was no different.

Grabbing a fist full of her fluffy hair, Damond took her until they were both slick with sweat. Slamming into her one last time, at last he came. yelling out into the silent house. Damond felt an unfamiliar peace as his eyes rolled back a bit, before they both slumped to the rug—exhausted but entirely satisfied.

Chapter Seventeen

The next week went by in a blur as they both hammered out work like crazy. Damond was extra moody those first few days as he fought his way to the end of book one. She'd patiently let his testier than normal attitude slide, and tried to cater to him until he finished. Like dropping food off in his office, so he wouldn't skip eating, and needling him to take a few much-needed breaks. Whenever normal measures didn't work she lured him away with sex. Once he'd typed the metaphoric "the end" they celebrated by taking that evening off after dinner. Playing downstairs, catching a movie before making love all night long.

They were doing that more often in fact, making love that is. As he started book two at a less frenzied pace, she finalized her work and their intimate time changed. Sex for them turned into long caresses, light touching, teasing kisses, giggles and sighs as hips met each other like they could spend all day at the activity. She loved it! But it also felt bittersweet.

But time didn't hold still, and even though they were both working less and spending more time together, her day to leave had arrived. She woke to breakfast in bed and ate it to please him even though she wasn't hungry. For Damond's part, he tried joking as a distraction, but Janae wasn't feeling their verbal sparring either. After a while he started getting just as distant as she was, before leaving to "take care of a few things".

At noon, she did a full sweep of the house, trying to make sure she hadn't left anything, only to end up almost crying at the memories in each space. Somehow she didn't, reality was standing on her doorstep and Professor Janae Williams Ph.D. didn't have time for tears, there was more work to be done.

Dragging her bags into the hall after putting on her coat, she ran upstairs to run her eyes over her office one more time *and* to avoid the inevitable. Damond knew she wanted to hit the road at 12:30 and it was almost that time. When she came back down he was waiting at the bottom step. Standing with his legs apart, hands stuffed in his sweatpants pockets, not much different than the first time she'd seen him fully dressed.

"Did you find anything up there?"

"No. I'm pretty sure I have everything."

"And if you don't, I'll make sure Amanda gets it back to you." Damond thought he was reassuring her. But the way her mouth dropped open before quickly closing told him he'd made some kind of misstep.

"Okay...thanks, I guess. I should be going, it's supposed to start snowing around six and I want to make sure I beat it. It could come early."

"Yeah, it might. You shouldn't have to stop, I mean gas wise."

"Thanks again for doing that." He'd gone into town yesterday morning and brought back enough gas to fill her tank.

"Don't let me hold you up Professor, drive safe." Damond nodded at her bags then looked at the door.

Janae's head snapped back at his blasé tone, gripping her keys so tight they hurt. "You're not even going to take my bags out to the car?"

"Why should I? You got them in here on your own, I figure you can get them out." Was she out of her social science loving mind? Damond didn't plan to lift *another* finger to help her leave here—leave *him*.

"Asshole," Janae muttered.

"What did you say?"

"I said you're an *ass-hole*." Janae fairly shouted in his face, her voice ripe with anger. "Was that clear enough for you?"

"Yeah, *that* I heard." He put his hands on his hips, just as pissed. "You ever wonder why?"

"I've concluded it's part of your DNA. I'm not sure I could figure it out, if I had all the time in the world Damond, and right now I have to go."

Janae turned away hurt. She hadn't expected some romantic movie of the week goodbye, but he could at least *pretend* he might miss her a little. Given her a damn hug.

"Or..." Damond broke into her thoughts. "You could stay another week."

Whipping around so fast she knocked over one of her bags, Janae gaped at him. "You know I can't do that!"

Damond only crossed his arms. "You can."

"My book-"

"Is in the editing stage. You can do that from here."

"True...but why should I?" Janae probed, even as her heart lifted.

"Because I want you to."

"Why should I care what you want?" Janae asked coolly.

"Because you want the same thing, to give us a little more time. One week, then we'll cut the strings and make a clean break."

Bundled in her thick winter coat she searched his face for answers. "Ask me to stay nicely."

He didn't hesitate. "Janae, please stay...give *us* one more week."

"Okay...just one more week." An unrestrained smile split her face as she embraced him. "But you're putting my luggage back in my room."

"You mean *our* room."

* * *

Over the next week they worked every day, but only five or six hours tops. The rest of the day they spent sleeping in, watching TV or movies. At one point she even let him try teaching her pool. Crazy as it sounded they took walks outside and had another snowball fight. Even competed to see who could make the best snowman in fifteen minutes. Janae won only because her decorations were better.

But just like the week before, it went by quicker than either of them wanted. She had gotten a call in the middle of the week from her parents who she had totally forgotten to inform about the extra time away. Then her cousin was leaving dire messages to give her a call "asap" when she returned. It looked like she was missed back in her real life. The morning of her second departure they woke to make love then repeated the act in the shower. Janae had so much sex in the last 48 hours, she was sure to be sore *long* after leaving.

Oddly, she was looking forward to that reminder of her time with Damond. But deja vu was starting to set in when she passed the suitcases in the hall this time around. When breakfast came to an end Janae looked across the table at the handsome, complicated, grumpy man sitting there.

"*Sooo*, I've been thinking, and maybe I want a few strings."

When he didn't say anything, she threw a strawberry at him.

"Damond, did you hear what I said?"

"Yeah, I heard you." He pushed back from the table only to stare. "You want to know the problem with strings Professor?"

"I don't, but tell me anyway."

"Strings are unwieldly and eventually get tangles. I don't like tangles."

"No one *likes* tangles." She gave him a perceptive look. "But if you handle the strings with care...you don't get pesky knots."

"See! Even you know it goes from tangles to knots, a downward spiral!"

"As much as I find this allegorical tennis match we're doing fun. I want to be clear. *I* don't want our relationship to completely end when I leave here. Now *you* tell me what you think about that."

Damond rubbed his jaw. "I think...things get hectic and complicated outside these cabin walls for two people like us."

"I agree. Complicated but not impossible...right?" Hope dripping in her voice.

He gave her a long searching look, and let out an even longer sigh. "I write fiction for a living. So no, nothing is impossible."

"Okay, what do you want to try?"

"I'm willing to keep a few strings going between us. Let's keep in contact, we can start there."

He wrote down his email and phone number on one of his prized notebook pages. She took it, gently folding it before putting it in her pocket.

"I think that's a great place to start. Let me go use the restroom and then I *really* do need to hit the road."

Coming out a few minutes later, her bags where gone.

"Look Damond, I don't have time to play. I need to get going. What did you do with my bags?"

"I took them out to the car, your purse too."

"Oh, that was nice."

Damond kissed the top of her head quickly before pushing her away.

"Get out of here, drive safe."

"Thanks." She quickly put on her coat, car keys in hand before turning back one last time.

Damond gave her a little wave. "Bye, Professor."

"I prefer *see you later*. Good luck on the rest of your work grumpy."

"You too."

She had known this was going to be hard and it was. Janae also knew they could keep this banter up all day. Without another word she walked out the door—closing it firmly shut.

Chapter Eighteen

Her drive back to Ann Arbor was overall uneventful. When she was about halfway there she put on her headset and dialed her cousin, who picked up right away.

"Hey lady! It's good to finally hear from you. I've been busting at the seams to talk! Didn't want to email or call while you were working. Did you get what you needed done?"

Janae frowned, Shella rarely babbled.

"I did actually! The book is done. That extra week was for fine tuning some things...plus I got sidetracked."

Did she want to tell her about Damond? Of course she did, but not while parting from him was still fresh. Shella took the choice from her anyway.

"I get it, I know how you get when you're focused on something important. But I really need to talk. I have something important of my own to tell you! Are you sitting down?"

"Technically, yes. I'm in the car." Janae laughed, finally recognizing the outright nerves in her cousin's voice. "What is it? Don't tell me you decided not to come back. That you'll be living in Spain or someplace."

At the silence that joke produced, Janae squinted out her windshield in disbelief. "Hello...Shella? Tell me you didn't do that."

"Noooo," she said slowly. "I mean I thought about it a time or two. You know what...I think I should tell you later."

"I don't think so. You've been pestering me to call. I'm sorry I put you off, but now I want to hear it."

"I just think you should be at home. I'd never forgive myself if my news made you run off the road."

"Wait a minute! What kind of news would make me do that? Spill it."

"I don't think I will." Her cousins' voice took on a playful note. "Look drive safe and let me know when you get home with a text. Then maybe we can do lunch tomorrow after you've had time to rest. How does that sound?"

"It sounds like you're stalling and now I *really* want to know what you're hiding."

"I'm not hiding anything, which is why we'll have lunch or even dinner if you prefer, *tomorrow*. Bye, and watch the road. Oh, and call your mama when you get in. Both your parents are driving me crazy. They think you've been kidnapped by some forest man and became his sex slave."

"Stop it!"

Janae spat out laughing. She knew her parents hadn't said anything like that, and that Shella was trying to deflect, which worked. It was extra funny since her cousin was close to the truth.

"I finally got in contact with them a few days ago, but I'll call as soon as I get in the door. I told them not to worry."

"Do parents ever stop worrying? Anyway, I'll see you tomorrow. Don't forget to let me know when you get home safe."

"Okay, okay. Talk to you later."

Janae hung up, entertained for the next hour by trying to guess her cousin's secret before it started to snow. Luckily, she had only an hour to go and was much closer to civilization. If it got really bad she could actually pull off at an exit. Turned out she didn't need to and Janae made it to her house ten minutes before five-thirty.

Lugging her suitcases inside her apartment, she left them in the doorway untouched. Janae was usually the type to unpack right away, but she just didn't have the energy, nor did she frankly care at the moment. Instead, she texted her cousin, then called her mom and dad. Talking to them both briefly before making an excuse to get off the phone.

With that out the way, she swapped her clothes for some fuzzy pj's before fixing herself a simple turkey sandwich for dinner. That made her think of Damond, it would be dinner time for him soon, he would be eating alone as well. Funny how she'd never been bothered by that before, the eating alone thing. It was her norm more often than not, but doing it now felt a bit bleak.

Deciding to zone out with some mindless TV she turned on Netflix, finding a comedy to make her laugh, and keep her mind off a certain man. But thirty minutes into the movie she debated with herself about texting him or not. Janae had transferred his information to her phone before starting the drive back, afraid she would lose the paper and have no way to keep in touch. After another few minutes of internal debate, she decided a brief text wouldn't be a big deal.

Janae: Just wanted to let you know I made it home about an hour and a half ago

She tried not to track the clock as she waited on him to reply, *if* he even would. After all, he might actually be working and she told herself it didn't matter either way. But when her phone pinged five minutes later, she fumbled to pick it up.

D. Hall: That's good...snow give you any trouble?
Janae: A little but I was almost home by that time
D. Hall: Good

Well crap, should she keep it going? Maybe it was best to keep it short for now.

Janae: Have a good night
D. Hall: You do the same

She twisted her lips, oddly dissatisfied with their conversation. It seemed dry to her, formal and obligatory. He hadn't made a joke, she hadn't tried to remind him of some menial task he should do. They'd both been flat. Janae tried to remind herself they were both dealing with this new reality of not being in the cabin anymore, and things would be different. They would have to wait, and see if it was *different* in a way that still worked for them.

* * *

Shella had ended up bringing brunch to Janae's house the day after she got back. Making her wait until they finished eating before telling her the news, and Janae *had* been glad to be sitting down. Her mind blown to the point where she needed a drink. They'd ended up talking for hours, until it was time for dinner so they ordered in. Both too distracted to cook.

Eventually, Janae shared her own travel secret as well. Telling Shella all about Damon and the rocky road from annoyed housemates to lovers. Shella was thrilled for her, but Janae shut her down quick, there was nothing to be "happy" about just yet. Damond and she had an interesting road ahead, as they tried to figure out if it had been cabin fever or something more. However, before Shella left she made Janae promise to come to dinner at her house soon.

Two weeks later Janae was returning from that dinner at her cousin's home, her heart a little heavy. She was speechless and frankly in awe. Shella's path was unconventional for *anyone*, much less a forty-year-old black woman from the Midwest, but Janae was behind her all the way. Her time with Damond had taught her not everything had to be planned out, or even make sense. Some things just *were*.

Once home Janae decided to take a bubble bath, something old fashioned for her generation. But she took one every once in a while to truly relax, just as she was doing now. Since that first awkward text, she and Damond communicated daily, usually briefly in the late evening around eight or nine o'clock. She knew he was being thoughtful due to her early bedtime schedule, as she was back to her normal ten p.m. lights out. Afterall, she wasn't up sexing a night owl of a man anymore.

After the first couple of times the tone of the texts had gotten more personable, less stiff you could say. A few jokes and smart aleck comments started flowing like normal. Like how a couple times a week he teased her not to molest herself while thinking about him.

Janae had initiated their first phone call a few days ago, needing to hear his voice. Strangely missing that irony and cynicism of his. When he'd picked up, they talked about how his second book was coming along, and how her editing was driving her crazy. She'd made them hang up after an hour, reminding him he had work to do. Janae had a feeling they would have talked all night.

Janae did her best to be mindful he had work. Which was why they rarely talked by phone and kept texts short. She understood he needed to concentrate, and if he was feeling anything like her, their distance was enough of a distraction. Getting out the tub, it hit her that he only had one more week to go before coming home. When that happened he would only be thirty minutes from her. There would be nothing keeping them apart...unless it was themselves.

After everything with Shella, Janae decided when he got back she wanted to really go for it. True, they would be different versions of themselves back in the real world. Yet here she was, still eager to learn this other Damond if it came to that. All she could do was cross her fingers he would be excited to learn about his "Professor" in her natural habitat as well.

Chapter Nineteen

It had been three long hellish weeks. That was the kindest way Damond could describe his time at the cabin without Janae. The first day she left he tried to write, but ended up staring mostly out the window. When he tried playing some ball in the basement that had been a major disappointed as memories ran through his head. He needed to talk to the other owners about putting a small workout space down there. A weight rack and maybe a punching bag. Neither would take up much space and would have provided him a much-needed outlet for his frustration.

Instead, he'd given up and tried to take a nap. Only to call himself every kind of fool when he couldn't bring himself to get back in the bed they'd shared. His little neat woman had actually made it up before leaving, but she hadn't changed the sheets. He bet they still smelled like her, like them together. For a few seconds he thought about sleeping somewhere else, but decided he wasn't going to let something so inane dictate his actions.

He'd stripped the bed, put on new sheets and proceeded to toss and turn for an hour before finally drifting off. Later that evening Damond had finally gotten his mind together enough to start writing, only to be fucked up again when she texted. Glad when she kept it short, as he was floundering on what to say. However, the simple act of speaking with her, if only through text had sharpened his energy. That boost led him to write for the rest of the night, falling into bed at three a.m. So exhausted even the ghost of Janae couldn't keep him awake.

His brain and resolve seemed to reboot the next day and he'd thrown himself into work. After all he was here to do a job, not pine after a woman. So his routine changed, becoming more like before Janae stepped through that cabin door, turning his life upside down. He slept, wrote and ate when he thought about it, and took a shit when needed. It worked for him, his story filling page after page on the screen. Stopping to research annoyed him but it was necessary and provided his wrists a break. He really needed to take time and learn how to dictate better. At the rate he was going he was sure to have arthritis in another few years. Another problem he didn't need.

In the moments where he didn't work himself to exhaustion, thoughts of his proper Professor snuck in. She wasn't his woman—hadn't been when she walked in the house, but damn sure *felt* like it when she walked out. Which was just nuts. They'd probably get sick of each other on their first date back in the real world. Chance had made them two people stuck together, who ended up making the best out of a weird situation. Damond tried to convince himself of this, as he figured she was doing the same at home. But it didn't stop the need to communicate with her each night.

Frankly he looked forward to their texts, it reassured him that she hadn't forgotten about him *yet*. Hadn't used her logic to erase his existence from her mind. If she was going to be stuck in his head, then he wanted to be stuck in hers. That's right, if he had to suffer so did she. Janae had been right, he was an asshole. One who when motivated would never play fair to get what he wanted. No matter how much he tried to talk himself out of it, Damond was starting to think what he *wanted* was Janae.

Tomorrow he was leaving, but tonight he was bone tired, elated and conflicted at the same time. The first person he thought to share all those emotions with was nearly five hours away and most likely sleep. Regardless, he picked up the phone anyway.

*

Janae was dressed for bed, actually even in it but she wasn't sleeping. She was doing something she rarely had time to do, reading for pleasure. A vacation romance called _Crashing In On Love_, that normally she would have spent the entire book scoffing at the situation. That was before her own recent experience. Now she found it romantic, possible and was rooting for the two island love birds to make it work somehow when they got home. Probably because it hit close to her real life situation. Janae might not end up with a happy ending, but damn it she wanted someone to, even if they were fictional characters.

Deciding that was enough for tonight, Janae turned off her kindle and the bedside light, right before her phone rang. Sitting up, one hand reached for the light and the other for her phone. Both excited and worried when she saw it was Damond calling at 11:30.

"Hey, is everything okay?"

"Yes mother, you worry entirely too much for someone your age. Now go pour yourself a glass of alcohol."

Despite his flippant words he sounded extra tired. "I wouldn't worry if you weren't calling me so late, which is unusual. What are we drinking to?"

"You ask so many questions, no wonder you're a psychologist."

"Fine, I'm going to get wine. What are you drinking?"

"I'm drinking coffee."

"This late at night? Damond, you know-"

"Don't start. I need it, I'm beat. I've been going since nine this morning. I ate once and only allowed myself three pee breaks."

"That was very magnanimous of you." He just grunted, so she left the phone on the bed while she ran to the kitchen. It only took a minute before she came back to the line, since she had a bottle open already. "Okay I have my drink, so tell me."

"I finished the book. Eighty-two thousand, five-hundred and thirty-two words. I don't think I've ever written a novel that quick before. It's rough and I'll need to do a harsh first revision, but it's done."

"That's wonderful!" Janae was so excited for him. "Congrats! That *is* a big deal. I'm proud of you for putting your head down and knocking it out."

Did his chest just tighten because a woman he'd known for a couple of months said she was proud of him? Naw, it couldn't be. "Thanks, I'm pretty pumped about it too."

"Well, you don't sound like it. Are you sure you're okay?"

"I worked myself to death since no one was here to distract me." Damond told the truth.

"Aww, you poor baby. But it will all be worth it in the end. Now you can launch your new series fairly close together, and this gives you a bit of a breather and time to write the next one. How many were you thinking would go in this series again, six?"

"At least. More if it does well. I'm hoping this becomes my signature series. Which if you look at the Alex Cross books, those have close to thirty. I'll definitely still branch out and do other stuff, but if you find yourself with a money maker you keep it going. Assuming you can keep the story fresh."

"True, some of my favorite cozy mystery series go on forever."

"Why does it not surprise me that you like watered down thrillers."

"Hey! To each their own. I'll let that go since you sound tired enough to be delusional."

"My bad, you're right it was unnecessary. You're also right on the other point. My eyes are crusty and heavy, if I start snoring in the middle of a sentence don't take it personally."

"I'll try not to. If you were so tired Damond, you should have gone straight to bed."

"No Professor, I had to tell somebody, and the first person that came to mind was *you*."

"Oh." She didn't know what to say to that, or what it implied. She just knew it made her feel special. "In that case I'm very happy you called."

"Me too." Damond sighed heavily. "I'll be heading home tomorrow, I want to see you."

Janae was glad she was sitting because the words made her weak. They'd talked about a lot of things, but not where their relationship was going. She was relieved he had brought it up.

"I'd really like that. But you sound like you need rest, a lot of it. And probably some real downtime even once you get back."

"I hate to say it, but you're right on the money again. I was thinking the weekend after next? We could go out for dinner...does that work for you?"

"It does," she replied quickly.

"Sure you don't want to check your schedule?"

"No." Janae's tone was serious. "It works, and if it doesn't I'll *make* it work."

Janae wanted him to understand she wanted this and was willing to put effort into it.

"That's what a man likes to hear. Do me a favor though, you pick a place."

"I don't care where we go I-"

"I know and neither do I. Pick a place that sounds good to you and let me know. I just can't bring my brain to focus on those kinds of details right now. As long as you show up, I don't care if we eat in a drive-thru."

She laughed softly. "Got it. Still, I'll try my hardest to do a little better than that. Damond..."

"Yeah, what?"

"I'm looking forward to seeing you again."

"Same here, and that makes four things I've agreed with you on tonight. I *must* be incoherent."

"Obviously." She was grinning ear to ear. "Get some rest, like immediately okay. Let me know when you arrive safe tomorrow."

"Can do. Good night Professor."

Hanging up, Janae finished the rest of her wine, doing a silent toast to his accomplishment. The conversation had her keyed up for several reasons, so maybe the alcohol would help her sleep. The validation that he wanted to still see her made her giddy. Soon she would be able to kiss his lips, be held in his strong arms and Janae couldn't freaking wait!

Chapter Twenty

The weeks flew by and before she knew it the Saturday date night had arrived! Janae picked a place in his city, making him joke it was because the food was better in Southfield, but that wasn't the reason. Janae was hoping the date would end in his bed, but *he* didn't need to know that. Her mother always said keep a man guessing, at least a little.

Truth be told, she was also curious about his place. A person's living style could tell you a lot about their personality. Your home was your solace after all, and her space defiantly reflected her simple taste. Decorated with clean lines and muted colors in most of the rooms, though her bathroom and office showed another side of her. Bright and even whimsical is how she would describe it. Her mother hated the stark contrast to the rest of the house, but that was neither here nor there. Her mind was focused on *literally* knocking the socks off of the man she was driving to meet.

Janae had declined his offer to pick her up, she was going to his spot tonight, not the other way around. Giving in to a hint of vainness she had went shopping for a dress just to impress him. Rationally she knew there was suitable stuff in her packed closet, but it was something empowering about buying something new that gave a woman confidence. The suggestive red drape dress gracing her body was just the thing to get her excited, and she was optimistic it would do the same for Damond.

It had a V-neck that was just *shy* of being scandalous and a surplice knot at the waist, drawing attention to the flair of her hips. The material was clingy but not skintight, moving with the motion of her body. She loved it! Shella had given it a thumbs up when Janae sent it to her before buying.

The dress was short sleeved which was a gamble with Michigan's April weather, but she did have a wrap in the car since most restaurants were chilly. She wanted to be sexy, not uncomfortable. Janae arrived early to Bacco Ristorante, nervous at the possibility of being late. Not wanting him to even *consider* she would stand him up.

She had lucked up on a spot in the front near the door, informing him that if he was nearby he might get the empty spot next to her. Less than a minute later his familiar car pulled in. Sending him a quick wave, Janae had no clue if he could see her through the heavily tinted windows. Why men liked to drive around like they were in the witness protection program she would never know. Stopping the rambling in her own head, Janae stepped out clutching her small purse. His back was to her for a moment as he got out and she held her breath as he walked over.

"Hi, Damond."

He didn't respond, just studied her from the three-inch heeled stiletto's to her bare legs, up over her fluttering stomach before lingering on her barely contained breasts.

"Fuck dinner." Were his first words of greeting.

"You know, I was thinking the same thing." She laughed, the tension broken even while a different kind took its place. "I *am* hungry...but not for anything in that restaurant."

Just then a light sprinkle of rain started to fall but neither reacted nor cared.

"You're getting all wet. Where's your umbrella?" Damond's voice was thick, taken over with lust.

"Doesn't matter, I was wet already anyway..."

He tried to snatch her close, but she evaded those talented hands. Knowing that once they touched, public decency would fly out the window.

"Damond, I really think we should go to your spot, before any contact takes place."

"You *are* a really smart lady. Follow me, I'm about ten minutes up the road."

* * *

Janae felt like a live wire as she followed close behind him on Ten Mile road. Apparently, he was as excited as she was because he ran a yellow light twice. She hoped neither of them got pulled over. Not worried about getting a ticket, she just didn't want to get delayed from getting to his bed, floor, couch— wherever they ended up.

She couldn't have written a better scene than what actually happened in that parking lot. She was like a junkie who had been clean for a few months, who suddenly came face to face with their addiction. Where the control you had stored up turned out to be nonexistent. Damond was apparently her drug of choice and she was getting a hit tonight no matter what!

Damond knew she probably thought he was a nut, running lights and taking corners fast. Honestly, he would have gone faster but he was afraid he'd lose her and didn't want to waste time giving directions. Shit, he just wanted to be inside her as soon as possible. Now he was glad for the condom in his pants pocket, even though it hadn't made sense at the time. It wasn't as if he planned to take her on the restaurant table, but hell, his intuition had been telling him it was better to be prepared than lose out on an opportunity.

He was hard enough right now to slide the prophylactic on, and considered doing it at the last light before his house. Would that make him a weirdo or just plain sprung? Like he had *zero mutha-fucking* self-control. Damond didn't really care what it said about him. He just didn't want to freak her out and ruin anything.

"Go for it, man."

Hyping himself up he did the deed, glad for his tinted windows so no one could see. Handling himself only made it worse as he struggled to get his willy *back* in his dress pants. Damond had never been so happy to pull into his condo as he was now, despite his brain having to remind his hand to put the car in park as it rolled a little.

"Get a grip." He mumbled to himself, watching her park.

With the thought to offer his suitcoat as protection against the rain he hurried over, but Janae stepped out with a wrap held over her head so he just took over the duty as he led her quickly to the door, but still the pair was damp by the time he ushered them in. The lock barely clicked before he threw his keys *and* her cape to the floor, spinning Janae around to claim the mouth he'd been missing in an all-consuming kiss.

They stumbled forward, both divesting themselves of shoes, while she pulled at his tie and attacked his shirt buttons. All in between her throaty laughter and his low growls, he managed to unzip her dress and unhook the bra without breaking the kiss. When at last her hand went to the front of his pants, they drew apart.

"Damond...you never said a proper hello to me." She squeezed his manhood softly.

"Baby, I'm about to give you the *only* hello that matters in just a few more seconds."

He steered her towards the bedroom between more kissing, groping and teasing. Once inside she rid him of his belt allowing his pants to fully drop. Damond kicked them away as her dress pooled to the floor and he pulled back in surprise.

"*You* don't have any damn panties on!" Shock vibrated in his voice.

"And *you* are somehow already strapped up." Janae observed. "I'd say we're about even."

Damond let out a laugh that came from his soul. This vibrant woman could match his wit and was never afraid to challenge him. Pulling her close again his hand parted her thighs to test her earlier statement. She was wet alright, and he was willing and ready.

"You are so fucking hot. So damn sexy."

Boosting her up until she wrapped those welcoming legs around him, Damond guided his cock to her opening and slid home. And by god, that's exactly what it felt like. Her walls shaping him like it had a memory. Making them both cry out in contentment at the long-awaited connection.

*

They didn't leave the bed for a *long* time, until finally Janae rolled over and groaned.

"I don't want to get up but the bathroom is calling."

"The hall to your right, first door."

"Thanks. Do you have a t-shirt I can slip on?"

"You don't need one, you're coming back to this bed."

"*I'd* like a shirt please." She said patiently, ignoring his tone.

"Use whatever you want, my dresser is right there." Damond scratched his chest. He was drained pun intended, but this time in a good way. They had worn each other out.

"Can you get it for me?"

"Let me get this straight." He looked at her like she was insane. "You want me to get out of bed to get you a shirt, so you can get out of bed. Is that right?"

"Yes."

"Why in the world would I do-"

"I'd like to go to the bathroom sometime this year please." Janae interrupted.

"Damnit." Mumbling he rolled out of bed, stomping over to the dresser.

He'd been dreading this, the moment she realized his ass was hooked. If tonight was any indication of what regular "outside cabin" Janae was like, then he was in trouble. Just look how she was ordering him about for idiotic stuff, but he wasn't going to roll over quietly. Tossing her one of his oversized shirts he took a figurative swing.

"Funny, since someone made me get up I suddenly have to use the bathroom myself."

"Damond!" Janae sputtered, rushing to pull the shirt on.

By the time she did he was long gone. Sighing with equal parts annoyance and amusement, she got up. Their reunion had exceeded her expectations, she loved how being around Damond made her feel. No other man so passionately wanted her, told and showed her that she was sexy. It was an ego boost that did wonders for her own sexual confidence *and* libido.

Walking to the kitchen on a quest for water, she quickly ran a glass from the tap. Parched wasn't a word that did justice to what she was feeling. The two had taken making up for lost time to another level. Janae would need to replenish all those calories burned. Which was why she was standing there looking in his fridge when he finally joined her.

"Damond, you should be ashamed at how empty this is."

"I just got back. I emptied it out before I left, so nothing would spoil."

"You're been back for *two* weeks."

"Yeah, but after a day of sleeping I got back to work. I have two books to revise, remember."

"I know but still," she insisted. "I'm hungry for food *now*."

"I'll order us something, what do you want? Most places deliver around here."

"I don't care. I'm going to the bathroom. You know what I like." Janae said while walking off.

Damond decided to order from a rib and chicken place that he knew delivered fast and tasted great. Making sure to get a salad too or she'd complain about not having anything healthy to eat. He *did* know his Janae. Well, he thought he did, until she came tonight looking like a siren the devil sent to torture him. When she came back wearing his shirt that looked like a nightgown on her, he thought about flipping it up and bending her over. Somehow, he managed to just relay what he'd ordered instead, getting a nod of approval at his choices.

"Will you show me around real quick? I'm curious to see the place."

As he walked her around, she became intrigued. Janae had expected all dark masculine colors and those were here but mixed with bright modern prints on the walls. His furniture even had a funky contemporary vibe going on. She liked it! It really expressed who he was. Daring, confident, creative but conversely muted at times.

"You did a great job decorating your place. It fits you."

"Thanks." Damond blew out a breath. "But I didn't pick most of it."

"Really? Who did?"

"Veronica." He said shortly, walking into the bedroom to finally throw on some clothes before the food came.

"Oh..."

"That sounded like a loaded *oh*, something on your mind?"

"Tell me about your relationship. How'd you meet? You never talked in detail about her at the cabin."

"Shit, Janae not much to tell. I met her on one of the rare times I went to a club with a few friends. We hit it off, started dating. Six months later she moved in and started changing everything. It looked good so I left it. That's it."

The knock on the door saved her from having to respond, and she let it go as they ate. But in her mind *six months* kept running through her head. He'd liked his ex-girlfriend enough to let her move in after only *six months*.

Chapter Twenty-One

Janae stayed the night and the next day, in which the only clothes she wore, were his various shirts. She didn't get into her dress again until Sunday evening when they finally had dinner at the original restaurant. The food was delicious, and she enjoyed ogling Damond in his dress clothes. The man cleaned up like nobody's business! He tried to get her to stay another night but she had her own work to do. Her book revisions had only been sent off to her editor recently, which put her behind on her class planning.

After prying herself away from his goodbye kiss, she finally went home. The month of May hit and they found themselves settling into a routine around her "Intro to Psychology" class which took place Monday, Wednesday and Friday. They usually met at least once during the week on one of her off days for lunch or dinner, often followed by some *quality* time. Every weekend found them shacking up at one of their homes. Damond had teased her mercilessly about her sunshine inspired bathroom the first time he'd seen it.

Along with classes and her relationship, she spent weeks accepting and denying changes from the editor. That was before looking over the entire thing again to make sure her corrections hadn't caused any *new* mistakes. A week and a half before June rolled in, she was sending the last draft off to the peer-review team and holding her breath for the outcome. Surprised when she got the input back fairly quickly, but also thankful because that meant as June was ending, her book was finally complete and she was able to send it off to the printers. Dr. Janae Williams, Ph.D. had a solo book to her name!

When she shared the news with Damond he insisted on taking her out to celebrate. Honestly, she would have preferred to stay home with him and relax with a movie, but she didn't want to diffuse his enthusiasm and it was nice to have someone besides her family to celebrate her success like their own. This time she picked McVee's, a place neither had to get really dressed up for. Though she put on a nice sundress that could work as casual or semi dressy. In the middle of dinner she flagged down their waiter and asked if they had any champagne on the menu. When it was brought to the table she turned to Damond.

"I want to make a toast." She was a little buzzed off the cocktails and it was starting to show.

"You do? This should be interesting."

"To us! Two authors who completed their books and didn't kill each other or anyone else."

"I'll drink to that." Damond clinked his glass against hers. "You know, that sounds like a good idea for a book."

Janae couldn't help rolling her eyes. "Everything sounds like a good idea for a book to you."

"The price you pay for dating a writer. Plus, don't act like I don't see you taking notes from time to time on folks, *me* mainly. We're fodder for each other's work."

"You're right, but at least all my research subjects are protected. The lawyers insist on it."

"Not mine. I've definitely killed off some real-life folks in my books. Now back to this killer writer. Think about it, every time he gets writer's block, he takes out his anger and aggression on some unsuspecting person. Or maybe only people who he thinks is stifling his creativity."

Janae loved hearing the excitement in his voice when a new idea grabbed his attention. He was like a kid who'd just discovered a new flavor of candy.

"Okay, but why can't it be a woman? I think she'd have more folks to be angry at. Her male competitors who don't take her seriously, publishers who undervalue her stories. Maybe even fans of her genre that give her a harder time than her counterparts. I got it! It can be an unreasonable bad review that sets her off the first time, in addition to the writer's block."

Damond stroked his chin in thought for a moment, leaning back in his chair. Then suddenly sat forward grabbing her hands across the table.

"See *this* is why I keep you around. That is a great twist. You get into the "why" of the killer's brain even more easily than I do."

"Thanks for the compliment...I think," she said drolly.

"You're welcome Professor."

Damond leaned over the table giving her a quick kiss, before sitting back and pulling out his pad to start writing notes. Janae shook her head and smiled before standing up.

"Let me leave you alone with your mistress. Going to the bathroom, be right back." Getting a nod in response she went off to do her business.

*

Damond knew Janae hated to see his notebook come out, but also knew she understood. Just like at the cabin he took it everywhere with him. He knew most authors used the recording function on their phones for spur of the moment ideas, or even the notes app. For whatever reason, he preferred hand writing them down. At the end of the day it didn't hurt, and gave him a chance to use that neat handwriting his mother had drilled into him.

137

The only time Damond was guaranteed *not* to let his mistress as Janae called it interrupt, was when they were getting down. Once they started on that path nothing distracted him from her. He was feeling really lucky tonight to have found someone who understood both him and his writing. While she may have thought a few things annoying, she made an effort to understand and accept that it was just part of his process. The total opposite of Veronica. That woman had complained about the time and focus his writing took from her, that the notebook made her feel in second place.

Their first serious "this might be the end fight" had occurred when Veronica had been sulking because he couldn't take her out one night, while he was working on the last few chapters of a book. The ideas had been damn near pouring out of his head, not only for the current book but for the next one in the series. He had been going back and forth from his notebook to his computer nonstop, until his near bursting bladder made him get up.

Returning from the bathroom he'd gone right back at it. Until ten minutes later another idea for the next book popped up and he reached for his notebook. When he hadn't been able to find it all hell broke loose. Veronica had taken it and after some yelling and even a threat or two, she had finally told him it was in the trash. Damond had retrieved it, packed his computer and a gym bag full of clothes and got the hell out of there.

It was the first time he'd ever felt like putting his hands on a woman. He should have known it would never work between them then and there. After two days in a hotel spent finishing the book and cooling off, he'd come home, a fool who thought himself in love. She'd been contrite with tears and all, promising to never do anything like that again and he'd forgiven her. Actually, that incident was why the notebook went even to the crapper with him.

"Hey, Damond."

What in the hell? Looking up he verified his ears had been right. Veronica in the flesh stood by the table.

"So, I guess it's true. People say you can think up the devil if you try hard enough."

Veronica ignored his barb and dropped into Janae's spot.

"How are you? I noticed you over here and decided to come say hi."

Veronica had noticed him alright, from when he first walked in with *that* woman. Had watched them all evening, eating off each other's plates, laughing and sending teasing looks at each other. Had seen that toast and kiss too, before whoever she was had scampered off.

"You've said hi, are you happy now? Are you still with Mr. Richie Rich?"

"You mean Calvin...and yes I am. Why do you ask, you trying to see if I'm available?"

Veronica sent him a flirty open look. Yeah, she was with Calvin, and his pockets were still a bit fatter than Damond's had been, but he lacked in other areas, mainly the bedroom. Damond won in that arena hands down, and after more than a year and a half of doing without the good stuff, seeing him tonight had reminded her where to get a hit that was sure to give her a high.

"Only thing I'm trying to see is why this conversation isn't over."

"Oh, don't be like that Damond. Are you saying we'd have more to talk about if Calvin wasn't in the picture?"

"Hell no!" Damond scoffed and stood up, which forced her to slowly do the same. "You're done with me remember? Gotta say that was the best decision you ever made for us both. I'm with someone else, which I have a feeling you already know."

Janae rounded the back of the booth at that exact moment.

"Hope I'm not interrupting." She asked the question of Damond, while keeping her eyes on the woman before her.

"Not one bit, she was just-"

"Wow...you *are* really tall." Janae cut him off stepping a little closer.

"Excuse me?" Veronica sniffed taking offense.

Damond snickered. Veronica was one of those odd women who didn't like their height. She had once told him she wanted to be shorter, more petite. He had chalked it up to her wanting to play the damsel in distress more convincingly.

Damond went to introduce them. "Janae this is-"

"Veronica. I've heard a bit about you, like the tall thing."

"I see. He was just telling me about you..."

"I gathered," Janae said curtly. "Are you here with a date?"

"No, just some friends. Actually, one of them pointed him out. They recognized him from the *years* we dated." She let out a fake laugh. "I hadn't seen him over here. Figured I'd come say a friendly hello."

"Hello," Janae said dismissively. "Goodbye. Don't let us keep you from your friends." Sliding around the other woman, Janae took her seat. Damond did the same, wisely not saying another word. Veronica gave a huff and flounced back to her table.

"That was interesting." He deadpanned.

"What? The conversation you two had?"

"Yeah that too, but I meant you. I'm impressed with your level of petty and vindictiveness. We make a good match."

Chapter Twenty-Two

The rest of the dinner went okay, but when Janae declined dessert Damond knew there was going to be a problem. He ordered cheesecake to go anyway, and that only earned him the pressed lips routine. He tried to let her be on the ride home, but his own temper started rising thinking about the vapid Veronica.

The night had been going great as they celebrated Janae's accomplishment, then Veronica had to bring her ass over. Damond knew damn well she'd seen he was with a date, probably watched them all night waiting for a chance to insert herself. Then having the gall to suggest they get back together or hook up! He'd read between all the lines, and had zero desire to catch anything she was throwing. At the end of the day Veronica had left him for a fatter cash cow and someone who had time to pander to her constantly. He would never, ever deal with her jaded ass again.

His joke, which really was an observation about Janae's pettiness, hadn't gone over well either. Didn't matter that *he* didn't see it as a flaw, the resident expert on human emotions seemed to hate anything that implied she had any of her own. Damond had liked knowing she felt territorial over him. He knew damn sure he would feel the same if some poindexter ex of hers had shown up. Still the entire dust up apparently had ruined Janae's mood, leaving it up to him to figure out a way to save the night. *Shit.*

*

"Hey, you sure you don't want any of this cheesecake?" Damond asked once they were in the house and settled.

"No, but if you want it you should have it. Don't deny yourself what you *really* want."

"Uh, okay." Sure was a lot of tone in her voice. "I didn't plan to *not* have any. I was just asking did *you* want some."

"I told you I didn't want any before you ordered it." Janae snapped, walking out the kitchen to go flop on the couch.

Damond put the container in the fridge, using his slipping patience not to slam it. Then he went and took a seat across from her.

"You can't be this annoyed about cheesecake."

"Maybe I am. You once again ignored what I said and did what you wanted to do. I didn't want any, you got it anyway. We're barely in the door before you try to make me have some."

"Now hold up a minute, *once again*? I've never ignored what you wanted and didn't this time either. I just knew you were trying to leave the restaurant as soon as possible, yet I also know you like sweets. Figured I'd get it so you could have it later, when you weren't pissed that an ex of mine spoke to me."

"I'm not pissed that your ex came to our table to flirt."

"Well, you sure as hell don't have all this attitude over damn *cheesecake*!"

Damond's voice raised, not quite shouting but not far from it, which didn't seem to help anything. If her mouth got any tighter she wouldn't have any lips, a hard feat for most black women to pull off. Collecting himself, he tried a different tactic.

"Talk to me, Professor, use your grown-up words."

He got a pillow to the face for that and more silence. Sitting back he waited. After about a full minute she looked over at him.

"I guess seeing Veronica didn't sit well with me. If I'm honest it ruined the night."

"I'm sorry. I wanted tonight to be about you. I had no clue she would be there. But this area is her normal stomping grounds. Or at least it was when we were together."

"I think she wants to get with you again." Janae said quietly.

"Who cares what she wants! What she wants is no longer any concern of mine. I can guarantee *I* don't want her."

"She's a real looker by the way."

Damond closed his eyes and bit his tongue to keep a flippant comment from coming out. He still ended up apparently mis-stepping.

"So, you're not going to dispute that." Janae accused.

"No. There's nothing to dispute. It's the first thing that caught my attention about Veronica. Besides I've been with a number of good-looking women in my lifetime, I'm with one now."

"Sure, but were they all your girlfriend?"

"What is that supposed to mean?"

Jesus, he hadn't had enough alcohol to deal with this shit tonight, or maybe he'd had too much.

"Come on Mr. Writer, you know words matter. When I came upon your little tetete you were telling her you were with *someone else*. Not with your new woman or girlfriend. Just *someone else*. Is that all I am to you?"

"Janae, don't do this. You're turning a conversation where I was telling her to kick rocks and making it into a negative."

"This isn't about her anymore, at least not directly. I know you weren't interested, I got that." Janae stood, crossing her arms too agitated to continue sitting. "You still haven't answered the question though. You do that when you don't want to talk about an issue. Just tell me, what am I to you?"

"Easy, you're my lover, my writing buddy. A friend and right now a pain in my ass." Damond stood as well. "Look, I'm sorry Veronica ruined your celebration. Let's not let a few minutes out of the entire night get us off track. Why don't we turn in early? We can watch a movie of your choice in bed."

Nodding her head, Janae turned on her heel marching to the bedroom. Damond waited a while, knowing that a silent woman after an argument meant it wasn't over. It only meant she had decided to let it go *for now*, but that it wasn't over in her head. This was going to be a long night, or more likely a short one if she decided to go to sleep. Damond took a deep breath, before heading down the hall to join her. Only to have her march pass him going in the opposite direction, her overnight bag clenched in a fist. Damond had to spin around to catch up.

"For real? Where are you going?" He couldn't believe this. "It's late, if you're that mad I'll sleep on the couch."

"Your *buddy* is going home to her own house." Janae grabbed her purse from the end table by the door. "This *friendly* visit is over."

"I don't call you the right term and that's it?"

"Yeah *lover*, that's it." And slamming out the door she was gone.

* * *

Janae drove home in a daze, ignoring the texts and calls from Damond that came in. When she finally arrived she just dumped everything carelessly by the door and got ready for bed. She had *never* been jealous like this before over a man. Disgusted when one was picked over her for a research team, even though she was more qualified *yes*, but over an ex-girlfriend *no*. Then again none of her other serious boyfriend's had ex's that looked like a model *and* was bold enough to approach him right in front of her either.

"The hell with her." Janae mumbled to an empty room.

She wasn't really upset about that part anymore just as she'd told Damond. He, nor she could control Veronica's actions. What the woman *had* done was remind Janae of something she had been trying to ignore. The designation of their relationship, and its projection. She hadn't forgotten that there was *something* about Veronica that had made him move the woman into his home so quickly. Or that their breakup hurt him bad enough that he'd been celibate and career driven for almost an entire year after.

She couldn't help but compare that to what she and Damond had now. They hadn't once talked about the future since they'd been back. Janae knew that going with the flow wasn't the worst thing and had been all for it while at the cabin. But that was then, not to mention a little slice of make believe. What they were, and if they had a future, were real *questions* that Janae wanted answers to.

There was little chance of her getting them tonight in any case. Too emotionally raw to have a rational conversation and outright pissed at the way Damond seemed to be so unconcerned of her feelings. So instead, Janae set her actual alarm clock and went to bed. Leaving her phone in the hall still in her purse. She didn't want to talk to him or anyone else right now.

*

Janae ignored him for the next couple of days, though she did text him once saying that she needed some space, but that they would talk soon. In the meantime she had done a lot of thinking. Reaching a conclusion she wasn't ready to face yet. It was July, and her summer class had started, which made the emotional strain she was under, physically draining too. Not that she was surprised by it, lethargy was a sign of depression after all.

Which is how Monday night while at home grading papers, she was caught off guard when her cell rang. The paper she was reading from a student was well thought out and distinctly interesting. Sadly, something that didn't happen as often as it should. So annoyed at being interrupted she answered without thinking about it.

"Hello, this is Janae."

"I'm glad. I'd be a little put off if someone else picked up."

"Damond...I wasn't expecting you."

"No doubt, or I'm sure you wouldn't have answered." He said flat out.

"Probably not," she agreed. "I'm grading papers right now. What can I help you with?"

"Janae, if you don't drop the professional office voice with me I'm going to get ticked off, and I called to talk not argue."

"Fine. What do you want?"

"What do I want? For starters I'd like to know why you walked out on me three days ago and have been ignoring my calls. Let's start there."

"I told you I needed a little space."

"We're better than this Professor. Let's not act like there's no issue to resolve."

"Don't call me Professor!"

It hurt to hear him use her nickname. She thought it had morphed into a term of affection. But now, maybe it was just an impersonal label he had for her.

"I have a name and I'm not so sure we're better than this. Haven't you called me petty and vindictive just recently, thought you liked it? Well, that's what you got."

Damond took a few deep breaths and tried to wrap his brain around what was happening. How his relationship had gone down the toilet so quickly and over nothing. Where the hell was all this coming from?

"Janae, I'm sorry. Whatever I did, or didn't do—I'm sorry. I want to talk this out and make it right. I want to fix it."

"Thanks for the blanket apology." Her voice lost its heat. Just sounding tired when she spoke next. "Look, you're partially right. I shouldn't have ignored you for this long. I really did need some time to think as I came to a decision. I've been avoiding having this conversation with you."

Damond's stomach dropped. "Why, what is it that you don't want to say? That I can tell I don't want to hear."

"Were done." Janae yanked the plug, pulling her heart out in the process.

"You don't mean that."

"I wish I didn't, but I do. We aren't going to work out. I looked at your past behaviors, plus mine and the evidence says we won't make it. We shouldn't waste any more time on this. We had a good run but-"

"Are you hearing yourself? A good run? What the hell! You sound like you're comparing what we have to the Popeye's chicken sandwich mania!" Damond laughed disbelievingly at what he was hearing. "Why are you throwing what we have away?"

"What do we have exactly? You couldn't tell me three days ago and you haven't explained it now. Because there are plenty of groups online where you can find a writing buddy. You can get a lover on some corners for forty bucks, hell many for free! As for friends, we're full-grown adults, we should have enough of those already."

Janae paused trying to control her voice as emotion took over. Steadying herself she finished what she had to do.

"I think this was eventually bound to happen. With us being on two different pages, hell maybe we weren't even reading from the same book. Sadly, I think our 'eventually' is now. As your lover-buddy-friend, I wish you continued success in your future endeavors. Goodbye, Damond."

Janae pressed the end button softly but firmly. Their story had come to an end. True, like all good books they left you wishing for more. But the reality was when a story was done— it was done.

Chapter Twenty-Three

Damond spent the next two weeks spiraling down into a funk. Folks never understood, but anyone who was a creative soul was most likely a sensitive one too. Now he didn't cry at the drop of a hat, but he shed tears. A *really* deep movie or book could get him going, shit he was human too. His eyes got a little moist at the news stories of abused pets and kids just like most normal people. Despite what Janae seemed to think, he wasn't devoid of feelings like his psychopath characters. Then again, hell if he knew what that woman was truly thinking anymore.

He was the same man she had met at the cabin, yet now he wasn't enough? He was starting to feel like he had the relationship version of PTSD. Veronica had left after finding what she bought into wasn't quite up to her standards, and now Janae—the hell with them. Now if only he meant it. Well, he did when it came to Veronica, but Damond wanted his little Professor back.

He'd all but stopped working and he damned himself for that. Hadn't he said after Veronica he would never let another woman affect his work again. But he just couldn't get his mind to act right or give a damn at the moment. Janae said she didn't want him, turning his sincere words against him. Was this another example of the differences in how men and women thought? Either way what could he do about it now?

He knew firsthand Janae could be stubborn. He was sure her tenacity was one of the reasons she'd gotten so far in life. But as he entered the third week of his pity party, his thinking shifted as he got the second book back from editing. He could be as stubborn as she was. Wasn't he the one that had scratched out a living by writing, a profession not considered stable or worthwhile by some.

Damond had fought his way into a genre dominated by white males *and* characters. Carving out his own space. Fought to find and grow his readership, and most recently battled his own thinking and trepidation in starting a new series. His mojo hadn't been gone, just his desire to pursue it. Meeting Janae had helped spark that fire in his writing *and* life. Yeah, he wasn't going to be kicked to the curb so easily this time, and if Professor Williams thought so, she had another thing coming.

* * *

Since she'd broken things off with Damond he hadn't called, texted or even emailed her. Hadn't put up any fight, and it made her incredibly sad. But that's what she had wanted—so that's what she got. It didn't change the fact that she missed him like crazy and cried herself to sleep a couple of times. But what was done was done, so she had no reason to screen her calls and picked up on a Thursday night to hear his familiar voice.

"Hey, Janae."

Took her a good five seconds to find her voice. "Damond...look if you-"

"Before you do your dial tone routine, I'm not calling about you and me. This is a business call."

"What business do we have?" Janae cleared her throat. "Not related to us."

"Writing. I need to consult with you again. I just got the edits back on the second book I wrote when you weren't there. I have some holes to shore up, things that need clarifying."

"You ever heard of Google?"

"See, come on don't be vindictive again. Look I'll find another head doctor to help me going forward, but right now you're all I've got. Aren't you all about social collaboration being the bedrock of a good society? I'm asking for one hour of your time. Maybe even less than that. I've made a list so I know exactly what I need to address. How about it?"

She gritted her teeth, hating that he'd called her out, hating even more the need to prove him wrong.

"Fine, an hour tops. Where do you want to meet?"

"I'd prefer to come to your place."

"I don't think that's necessary." Janae put frost in her tone.

"Look, call me crazy but I'm paranoid about talking in depth about my work out in public. You can't tell me you and yours don't keep your projects and research private for as long as possible, so others don't steal your shit?"

"I know you're exaggerating all this, just so you know. One hour, my house tomorrow at seven. I want to get this done and over with. If the time doesn't work for you then to bad."

"Oh, it works for me, and if it didn't work...I would make it work. See you tomorrow."

Damond disconnected from her this time, and she wasn't oblivious to the words she'd once spoken to him being thrown back at her. Reminding Janae that when she'd said it, it was to prove her commitment to starting a relationship with him.

* * *

Janae had no reason to be nervous about seeing him, so why was she? This was a brief business matter between them. After that she would never have to see or speak to him again. So why was she straightening up small things around the house, a pillow here, a picture there.

"Stop it Janae, this isn't a ladies brunch visit."

Funny she was worrying about the house, while for her appearance she had purposely dressed down. Didn't want him to mistake that she was trying to gain his attention. Her hair was pulled back into the severe bun he hated, with a full sleeve non-fitted shirt that was almost too hot for this time of the year. She was also determined to be polite and distant, just like any other business meeting. Her overthinking was cut short as he knocked on her door exactly at seven. *Here we go.*

"Damond. Thanks for being on time, come on in."

He did and she noticed he was wearing jeans and a faded t-shirt. Looked like he wasn't trying to impress her either.

"Thanks. Let's get down to business so I can get out of your hair."

"Okay...have a seat. Wait, where are your notes or laptop?" She asked, just noticing the obvious.

"I got everything I need right here." Damond pulled out his small notebook and a pen from his back pocket.

"This is ridiculous." She hurried to her office and got a legal pad. Slapping it on the table as she sat back down. "Here, use this. Because if you run out of room or whatever I don't want you saying we need to meet again. This is our *last* time seeing each other."

"Naw, I'm good." Damond tapped the book on his knee. "Now would you please be quiet while I explain what I need."

"By all means, the floor is yours," Janae stiffly replied.

"This character is a man who has a warped since of reality. He hurts people because he's been hurt, but in his mind he's never harmed anyone. He was rejected after a long time of living in a fantasy that was never real, and so he has a strong aversion of ever being caught up in that type of situation again. Every time he feels like things might be too good to be true, he lashes out and hurts someone else.

"Hmm, sounds like he may have a dissociative personality disorder, brought on by emotional distress." Janae's brow furrowed as she thought on it. "Though it was most likely a build up over time, and the last big rejection set him down this path of pushing folks away."

"I knew you'd understand." Damond smiled sadly. "Janae, that man is me."

"What? Are you playing some kind of game? I don't have time for this. You lied so you could see me."

She rose off the couch, only to have him gently take hold of her wrist.

"Are you really surprised I lied? Please sit and listen. Veronica was a fantasy for me, good looking and someone who needed me. She can play the *in need of saving* role pretty well when she wants, and from time to time *I* apparently like to play the knight in shining armor. She hoodwinked me, hell maybe I did it to myself. She needed support, money wise more than anything else. She never loved me and at the time I honestly thought I loved her. *That* was the rejection that broke this camel's back."

Janae slowly sat, pulling her arm away. "Go on."

"Just as you thought about the fictional character that wasn't the first rejection. Remember, I'd originally tried to go the route of being traditionally published for a few years before striking out as an indie. I got a ton of rejection letters, told that my books didn't fit solidly into one genre or the next. That my characters were too much and that while having a black lead was basically okay, no one wanted to read about black psychopaths or black folks and supernatural evil. It was always *something* and always *no*. Then right before Veronica left my sales were starting to plateau, all of it making me feel I wasn't good enough. Can you relate to ever feeling that way?"

Janae reached out to hold his hand. "Yes, more than once."

"I was up at that cabin just like you, trying to reinvent myself, taking a risk. I wasn't expecting you, wasn't ready for you Janae. Yet, I'm so thankful you were there. I wouldn't take that time back no matter what comes next."

"God, I wouldn't either." Janae had to lower her eyes, she couldn't look at him, but then thought she owed it to them both to face this head on. "I thought we had something unique and special. Damond...it hurt to find out we didn't."

"But we do! Which is why I can't wrap my mind around why you want to throw it away."

"I don't!" Janae pulled her hand back. "I get it, Veronica may have been a fantasy to you, but you still felt strongly enough about her to combine your lives after a measly six months. But with me, after the same amount of time, you can't even call me your girlfriend to another person. Hell, or even tell it to *me*. I wanted to mean more to you than just "someone else." Some interchangeable woman you happen to have in your life at the moment."

"I'm sorry I was so dense and made you feel that way. That was never my intention Janae. Part of me didn't want to rush into anything like I'd done with her, the other part was fear. Fear that I was a temporary curiosity for *you* and that you would wake up one day and tell me playtime was over. So I just let things ride, didn't want to rock the boat. I'm sorry, for not telling you sooner how I felt."

"Damond, you still haven't told me. What do you feel for me?"

"Well, that's why I bought my dependable notebook along." He finally opened the pintsize thing. "I know you were not thrilled with the way I described what you meant to me at my place."

"That's an understatement." She chuckled. "But yeah, it didn't make me happy."

"I think it's a case of "Men are from Mars, Women are from Venus" theory. You know differences in how we communicate."

Rolling her eyes Janae sent him an amused smile. "Can't wait to see how you equate our argument to this."

"Here me out, it's not farfetched. What's important to a man and how he expresses it may be different than how *you* would, but it doesn't mean the connotation behind it isn't the same."

He showed her a page in his book that simply had "lover" written in the middle.

"I called you my lover, not my hookup, not a sex partner, not some random person who as benefit of our acquaintance sex is had. The root word of lover is *love,* Janae. The way we connect physically has been more powerful than what I've ever experienced with any other woman. It was never "just" sex for me. What we did was making love regardless of the form it took."

"Damn you." She was leaking already. Trying to shake the tears from her face when he reached out a hand that knew every inch of her body, and gently wiped them away.

"Language Professor."

When she snorted a little at their running joke, he turned another page. This one had "writing buddy" on it.

"Speaking of language, the second thing I called you was my writing buddy. As you said words are important, and you and me understand each other's language. You were able to be yourself and so was I. You understood that my needling was a form of play, that my bark was bigger than my bite. Recognized my challenging comments were meant to provoke debate, because *I* like learning and exploring new ideas. That my mind was worthy of having deep, complex conversations.

And yes, it's also directly about writing too. Until I met you I'd never had a woman by my side who understood *a tenth* of what went into writing, how hard and stressful it could be. But with you, *you* got it. I think you can agree we're both better writers having the support system we provide each other."

"I suppose you're right. I figured out you weren't really a lone wolf a while ago."

"Come on, you know wolves are pack animals. The rare lone wolf is that way by circumstances not choice. And when he finds a mate they stay together for life. I have no desire to stay alone Janae. I want to be with you."

"Damond I-"

"No, I'm not done. You made a big deal about this and I want to address all of it."

"Fine, *now* you want to be precise. Go on then."

"The last word I called you was my friend." He turned another page to display the word. "Now I had to scratch my head at how you turned this globally positive word into a negative. Calling someone a friend is a huge compliment. I know it's been watered down by having 500 Facebook "friends" and shit like that. But when a man considers a woman his friend, he's elevated her from just a mere sex partner or something to do on the weekend. We shared our dreams, our doubts. The deeply personal things that make up our personalities. Friendship on top of everything else we have, is icing on the cake.

Real friendship is invaluable. It's when you know that through thick or thin a person will be there for you when it matters. That's how I knew you would see me today. You care about me as a person. You want to see my work succeed. Lifelong commitment takes more than just heat, it takes understanding and *friendship* too. That's what those three words I called you meant in *my* head."

Janae hesitated, catching her breath as the tears started again. "Is that what you want us to have, a lifelong commitment?"

"God, yes! That's what I just said woman. Get it through your thick head that I love you."

She threw herself in his arms, hugging him tight and being squeezed to death in return.

"I love you too! *You're* the thick headed one. If you had *just* said those three words in the first place, we wouldn't have had to go through this."

Damond laughed impishly, shaking a finger back and forth.

"Lady, I'm a writer. You know I had to express myself separately from those overused cliché words."

"Well, as a writer you also know that sometimes *clichés* are used so much because they work! It's what the readers want and understand."

"Wait, let me write that down." He turned to a clean page and wrote *I love you Janae*. "Now this notebook really has everything I need in it. How about a compromise? I promise to bring my artistic side down to your level and say those three words at least once a week, if you agree to come back to me and never leave again."

Janae palmed his face lovingly. "Make it twice a week and you have a deal, Mr. Hall."

"Done."

When she sealed it with a kiss, Damond was hard pressed not to let it get out of control, but his need to make sure they were on the same page came first.

"Janae, I want to be crystal clear on this. I want to collaborate in this thing called love and life with you. Is that what you want?

"It is. Damond, I love you. As long as we work together to make this love strong, anything we do in life will succeed."

"Amen to that Professor."

Epilogue

It was mid-December and winter had come on time this year. They'd had three big snow storms already and another was predicted for next week. Today was cold but at least it was snow free, which meant people weren't hesitating to come out this Saturday. This was a good thing, otherwise she would look stupid just sitting here.

Janae was in the Barnes & Noble in Ann Arbor having her first ever book signing. The book she had procrastinated over, stressed over and cried over had become an unusual surprise success. It seemed her time at the cabin had influenced how she wrote, and instead of the usually cold and clinical book that academics and students alike were used to, hers ended up being more humanized and contemporary.

Her peers, almost across the board had given it glowing reviews. Then a certain someone had used his connections to get her a segment on Fox 2 news, so she could talk about how her book could be used to understand some of the factors that played into aggression. Where programs in the community should focus their resources to mitigate risks, before it was too late to change behavior.

That eight minutes on air had inquiries from places she never imagined coming her way. Regular citizens had started buying the book, and various professors at a wide variety of schools were choosing to use it for their winter classes. So next month thousands of students would be forced to buy it. It was crazy! She'd gotten job offers from the bigger universities in the state, as well as a few across the country. For now, she was staying where she was at, but had a lot of thinking to do. A position at UofM didn't have many down sides, and she wouldn't have to uproot her entire life.

Janae was under no illusions, and knew this fame would be short lived, but she'd take it for as long as she could. Speaking of fame, she wasn't the only one who was getting some accolades or having a book signing today. Across the store there was an author who had a much more steady line of people than her, whose name happened to be Damond Hall. His new series *had* been the one to take his writing to that next level. The second book had released two weeks ago to even higher sales than the first. Word of mouth and his own news segment had helped. Like he'd suspected, people loved thrillers that focused on a main detective trying to stop the crazies.

When a store associate came and told her it was time for a brief break, she was relieved. She had ten minutes to use the bathroom, stuff something in her face and stretch her legs. Janae used the last few minutes talking to Damond when he approached her in a semi private corner.

"I've had more of a line than you all day Professor." Damon stated.

"I'm aware and it's not rocket science that more people would be interested in your book than mine. Frankly, I'm still astounded *anyone* showed up for me."

"I'm not. Makes sense my woman's work would be acknowledged, just like her man's."

"Your woman?" Janae poked him in his shoulder. "May I remind you I'm an accomplished psychologist in my own right."

"Don't I know it. It's because of you that my books are so good. Why don't you come on over and I can introduce the fans to uptight, straight-laced but sexy, Dr. Young. They'd flip out to see who the fictional character was based off."

"No way! Remember we said I'd consult as long as no one knew." Janae straightened her suit collar. "Umm, do readers really think the doctor is hot?"

"Hell yeah, and so do I. Half the emails I get are asking when the MC's get together *or* when I'm killing her off. Most mention she has that untapped heat to her."

"Really." Janae couldn't help grinning at that.

"Look at you, eating it up." Damon laughed amused. "You bookish types are always secretly looking for danger and excitement. I bet it turns you on knowing people might be lusting after you."

"Maybe." Janae discreetly grabbed his ass. "You'll have to wait until we get home and find out"

Damond being Damond didn't give a damn about discretion, bending down to give her a *more* than brief kiss on the lips.

"Later Professor, I can't wait."

She watched his squeezable ass walk back to his station before heading to hers. Home was a new three-bedroom split level condo in Ypsilanti on the lake. Cheaper than getting something in Ann Arbor, though not by much. Damond had moved out her way, seeing as she was the one that didn't work from home. They'd both sold or donated items they wanted to leave behind, integrating the other things that spoke to who they were in their shared space.

They were a team now, in so many ways. Working together on his books, living and loving life together. It was crazy to think that not quite a year ago she'd taken a gamble. Driving up in the wilderness during the dead of winter, looking for direction and inspiration. What she'd found was love and a brand new outlook on life. Their little lover's hiatus had been just the first chapter of what she hoped was a very long, glorious book.

Thank you for reading my work! I hope you enjoyed. Please support independent authors by leaving a review on the outlet of your purchase.